Normbies!

a collection by

David J. Lovato

A Brief Word on Order

While several of the stories in this collection are directly related to each other and take place in chronological order, the majority of them are not and do not.

These stories are set before, during, and after the discovery that biting zombies changes them back into people. The stories that follow each other linearly will be obvious, the rest have been ordered for pacing and flow, and not in order of when they occurred.

Table of Contents

Patient Zero

The toilet seat screamed when Billy lifted it, echoing along the halls and coming back like a misheard rumor, off-key and quiet. He listened to see if anything would notice, but didn't expect much; he had already checked the bottom floor thoroughly and found it empty.

Billy unzipped his pants and almost opened fire, then noticed the tail of toilet paper hanging from the roll set in the wall, disturbingly close to the toilet. He stepped to the side a little to block any splashback from hitting the exposed toilet paper, then chuckled to himself and let loose. Old habits die hard, even in the zombie apocalypse.

He knew it wouldn't flush so he didn't bother trying. Billy looked at himself, ripply in the old mirror, and said, "Dear Diary: Today I pissed in a toilet like the old days. It was wonderful."

He ran a cursory check for any food in the kitchen and found nothing. A glance through the kitchen window told him it would rain soon, so Billy decided this was as good a place as any to hunker down for the night. He unlocked the sliding glass back door, walked out from under the awning, then set up his raincatcher: A jug that would catch rainwater through a homemade filter, weighted down so it wouldn't tip over no matter what the wind threw at it. After that, Billy went back inside and locked the door behind him.

The house creaked and groaned with every step. He was wary of going up the stairs, but after the first few didn't give, he judged them structurally sound and ascended the stairs while whistling a tune. When he realized it was "Soul Meets Body" by Death Cab for Cutie, he stopped humming, stopped walking, stopped everything. The wind rustled outside, it whistled through a few loose boards somewhere in the attic, then Billy dried his eyes and headed down the upstairs hall.

The upstairs bedrooms looked the same as the first floor: Dusty furniture, toys strewn across a child's room, clothes hanging in closets, electronics so old they wouldn't turn on anymore. No survivors and no zombies, but whether there were ghosts was up for debate. The darkening sky let in little light, and Billy got the creeps and headed back downstairs.

It was sprinkling when he went through the back yard. The raincatcher was doing its job, but that wasn't why he was here. In a patch of grass far from the house, near the fence separating the yard from the neighbor's, he found tiny red strawberries growing under clovers. Billy picked as many as he could and put them in a baggie, ate a few of them (they had no flavor, but he was hungry) and then headed inside as the raindrops grew larger.

What little sun broke through the clouds disappeared as night fell. It was pitch black in the house, disturbed only by the lightning and the glow of the fireplace. Billy staved off his hunger as long as he could, and finally he cooked a can of beans in a pot he pulled from the kitchen (he preferred to use his own as seldom as possible, to avoid wear and tear).

He was lucky to have found a suburb mostly empty of zombies before the storm rolled in; weathering storms was difficult, and the rain didn't slow the zombies much, so sleep was a bad idea when it was even possible. Houses were always risky, but when it came to storms it was a risk worth taking, and this particular storm was a doozy.

After dinner Billy stripped naked and went outside, pressing through the wind and rain to get the raincatcher, which had filled up. He brought it inside and filled all of his skins and bottles, then braved the storm again to set the device back in the yard. After that he huddled as close to the fire as he could until he was dry, then dressed himself and made a bed out of blankets from the bedrooms. He couldn't use any from the child's room; the blood splatters, though they had long since dried, bothered him too much. It wasn't that cold, in any case.

In the morning the rain was still coming down, but it was much lighter. The sky was white and gave no signs of clearing up, so Billy stayed another day in the old house.

In the afternoon he counted his food: One more can of beans, two cans of peaches, and a few granola bars. He opened one of these and found it infested with some kind of larva, but he couldn't afford to discard it. Billy ate the granola bar with his eyes closed and his breath held.

That night he ate most of the berries, as they would spoil faster than the granola bars and the food in his cans. He slept in the house again, and in the morning he went out to collect his raincatcher. The ground around it was trampled in, almost like footprints. It must've rained hard. He gathered it up and headed out the front door of the house.

"You never get used to the weight," he said, shifting his backpack higher onto his shoulder. Anything that wasn't absolutely necessary had to be left behind, but you would be surprised how many things were absolutely necessary, and how much they weighed.

Everything had to be packed in as tightly as possible to avoid it clanking around and making noise, which meant extra effort whenever he had to take something out. Things like his main canteen and the granola bars were kept in easy-to-reach spots, things like the cans of food and ammo were a journey away.

Ahead he saw a figure and knelt behind a car. He took his backpack off and set it down while he pulled a crowbar from his belt loop. Thunder rolled in the distance, and Billy hoped it was an echo of the storm that had already passed and not another one coming to put him off gathering for another night or two.

The thing ahead shuffled back and forth in the road. Billy moved out from behind the car and knelt behind one a little closer, giving him a better view of the zombie.

It was missing an arm, and its jaw hung open, swinging up and down slightly but crooked when top met bottom; someone had run into this zombie and broken its jaw, but failed to give it the final blow. Without a sound Billy slipped the goggles around his neck over his eyes, rushed out from behind the car, and finished the job for them, plunging the crowbar deep into the creature's eye. Blood splattered across his goggles, but not enough to obstruct his view. With the crowbar he guided the zombie backward onto the street, then yanked the metal shaft out of its head. The zombie's eyeball stuck to the end of it, and Billy thrust it into the zombie's head another two times for good measure.

Billy wiped off the crowbar with the zombie's shirt (it was grungy but did the trick). He took his goggles from his face and let them rest against his chest, checked the dearly departed for anything useful, found nothing , and headed back toward his backpack.

He was tired from giving the zombie a brain-mashing, and when he picked up his pack, the weight of it nearly pulled him down. He hoisted the thing onto his back, using the car to hold himself up, and started along the road again. What felt like ten minutes later, he passed the zombie he had killed.

"Might be time to re-define 'absolutely necessary'," Billy muttered.

He walked for a few hours before rain began to fall, and the last thing he wanted was to be made even heavier by wet clothes. He recalled a summer or two before when it barely rained at all, and he once spent days lying on the ground near his raincatcher, slowly dying of thirst. Now he had more water than he could carry; if only he could travel through time and give Past Billy a glass of water.

If I could go back in time maybe I could prevent all this from even happening.

That seemed less likely; as far as he could tell, nobody understood what happened, or even when. He remembered things on the news, stories of people biting each other, some unknown contagion, but that was all so long ago, and didn't matter. A year into the apocalypse he had found a shed owned by a doomsday prepper, and all of the doomsday prepping in the world hadn't saved the old man from the mudslide that toppled his house, his shed, and crushed him below rocks and shrubs. Billy had found the guy only three feet from his stash of water, reaching for it but unable to get at any, unable to find enough leverage to free himself, and the whole thing was what convinced Billy to always be on the move.

He crossed the front yard of a house, cupped his ear against the door, and listened. The rain made it difficult to hear anything. He went to the nearest window and tried to open it, but found it locked. He checked the perimeter and found no unlocked windows or doors, which was both good and bad. There was probably food inside. There were probably zombies inside as well.

Billy let his backpack slump to the porch, grateful to be free of the weight. He climbed a nearby tree, crossed from its branches onto a small awning, and held onto the gutter while he leaned to the side and smashed in a second-floor window with his crowbar. He waited and listened, heard nothing but rain, and hoisted himself into the house, careful to avoid the glass.

He was in an empty bedroom. Clothes lay carelessly discarded, the drawers open and the closet door ajar. The bedroom door was open as well, and Billy crept to it, then glanced down the hall. The rest of the doors were shut. He went downstairs quietly, always listening for movement, always finding silence, and unlocked the front door. He dragged his backpack into the house (far too tired now to bother carrying it) and closed and locked the door behind him.

Billy found a small dresser near the door, upended the drawers, then smashed them into pieces. He looked at his little pile of wood and smashed the rest of the dresser too, for good measure. He set the wood down near the fireplace and set to work building a fire. Rain dripped down the chimney, but not enough to disturb the flames.

With some warmth coming in, Billy headed for the kitchen to look for food. The cupboards were also ajar, and most of them were empty, with dishes scattered across the floor and counters. A pot in the sink had been used to make spaghetti, and the homeowner had apparently not washed it before abandoning the house to the apocalypse, because maggots crawled in and out of the remains of the food. Billy sighed and collected them all in a tiny jar; he could eat them, but not while they were alive. He'd done it four times and found eating them dead was the only way to keep them down.

The food in the fridge was long-rotten, but he found a half-empty jar of peanut butter in a cupboard. Oil had collected on top, but he mixed it around with a knife, licked the knife clean, then tossed it into the sink. The cupboard also held a small box of ramen noodles; the world Billy came from held things like gold, oil, and six-inch strips of green paper in the highest esteem, but the world he found himself in now saved that pedestal only for ramen noodles. The fuckers never spoiled, weighed nothing, could be cooked anywhere, and tasted like angel hair. He would finish his berries tonight, but there were a dozen packets of noodles in the box, so he decided he would have one of those as well.

Since he would be using water for his noodles, Billy set his raincatcher up in the back yard, then came back inside to find something to cook them in. Pots were handy but not absolutely necessary, and he didn't carry one with him. The only one in the house was the spaghetti pot, so he did his best to scrape the years-old pasta out before he put much finer years-old pasta inside.

Billy set the noodles up to cook, then went exploring. There was a basement, but the shelves held only tools and car parts. There was a small pile of firewood in the corner, and Billy held a momentary vigil for the dresser he hadn't needed to smash to bits, then headed back upstairs.

The ground floor yielded little else of use. He managed to shave in the bathroom, rinsed himself off by sticking his head out the window, and sharpened his knife on a sharpener he found in the kitchen. He went upstairs to check the rest of the bedrooms for clothes; two of his three pairs of socks were wearing thin, and he could afford to swap out his shoes.

He started in the bedroom he'd come in through. Rain splashed in through the window, and when he searched it for clothes his size but found none, he closed the bedroom door to keep the cold in there. He tried the next door and found a teenage girl's room. Billy was never a big man, and the girl's custom My Little Pony Chuck Taylors fit like a glove. Or like shoes. Billy wasn't picky before the world ended and he certainly wasn't picky now.

Next up was a closet between bedrooms. Billy turned the knob, but never had a chance to pull on the door. It shoved toward him hard enough to knock him backward, make him drop his new shoes, and a zombie shouted "Yeeee-alch!" as it came tumbling out on top of him. As he landed on his back he noticed the blood stains on the carpet, the small red droplets here and there, and the dents in the door frame. He had been careless, but he didn't have time to learn his lesson; the zombie landed on top of him and bit into his shoulder.

"Fuck!" Billy screamed. He reached for his crowbar, but it was tangled in his belt loop below him. He punched the zombie in the side of its head, which did nothing at all to deter it from its meal. The zombie sank its teeth deeper into him, the pressure was unbearable. He beat at its head over and over again, but zombies feel no pain. The creature writhed as it clamped down, pushing its hands against his chest and head, then pushed against Billy's face, one scrawny pointer finger in his mouth, pulling against his cheek. Trying not to choke, Billy bit down as hard as he could. The zombie still felt nothing, but his teeth severed its finger, and the zombie's hand slid free of his face.

Billy spat the finger out, put a hand on either side of the zombie's head, and squeezed, hoping to crush its skull, but that was much harder than it sounded in his mind. He was able to yank it free of his shoulder, but not without a chunk of skin clinging to the creature's teeth. He realized he was screaming, and pain shot up his arm while blood squirted down it and onto the carpet.

With both feet Billy shoved the zombie back toward the closet. It slammed into the shelves inside, knocking one loose, which clattered onto his legs. Billy was already sitting up, clutching his shoulder, scrambling backward only to find the wall of the hallway. He dragged his legs out from under the shelf and shoved it forward, putting the shelf between him and the zombie, and with his back against the wall, he was able to prop them both in place. The zombie reached and reached, but while it clawed at his jeans, it had worn its nails down on the inside of the door who knew how long before. It leaned forward hoping to get a bite, and if the zombie's former self had been a practitioner of yoga, it might have been able to. Emaciated as it was, it couldn't lean forward enough to bite him.

The crowbar was pinned under Billy's ass. He tried to shift to get at it, but the shelf moved and the zombie nearly pushed free. Billy leaned back into the shelf, pinning the monster down again.

Outside, the rain beat against the house, and soon only the lightning was enough to illuminate the hallway. With each flash Billy saw those lifeless eyes, the effortless grasping at his legs, the teeth clacking together. He felt tired, like he was falling asleep. To add insult to injury, the smell of ramen noodles permeated the house. Billy found himself slipping several times, nearly letting the zombie free. He was fading away, he was almost over. Lightning struck nearby, jarring him a little more conscious, and he realized the zombie was no longer moving, like it had nodded off.

"Fuck you," Billy said.

"What?" the zombie replied, and lifted its head. It looked at Billy, squinting through the darkness, its eyes wide and darting around, full of fear.

Billy laughed and laughed. The zombie pushed the board away easily, and he was far too tired to hold it back anymore. It stood up before him in the hall.

"Oh my God," it said. He couldn't tell before, but it was a young woman. "I bit you, didn't I? I remember it. I remember everything."

"It's okay," Billy said. "I bit you back." Then he lost consciousness.

It was morning when Billy woke up. He was wrapped in blankets on the couch, and the fire in the fireplace was down to cinders. He heard something moving around, and sat up as quickly as he could. His shoulder hurt, and he realized it had been bandaged.

Billy scrambled to his feet and reached for his crowbar when the zombie from the night before entered the room. She was cleaner now, wearing different clothes, her missing finger gauzed off, and while she was still dangerously skinny, she had color in her, she was alive. She was also offering him a bowl of ramen noodles.

"It's okay," she said. Billy was still scrambling for the crowbar, but it wasn't there. "Your stuff is by your bag, it's over there. Eat these, I made them for you. I ate your berries, though."

"You're alive," Billy said. "You were one of them, you were a zombie."

"I remember being in that closet," the woman replied. "That's all. So long, just scratching at the door, trying the knob, I couldn't even turn around because of the shelves. And I remember trying to…" she looked at the floor. "Trying to eat you. I wanted to eat you so badly."

"You almost did." Billy took the bowl from her, sat down, and started eating. "You look hungrier than me."

"I'm starving. But I don't want to eat too fast. I heard it can rupture your stomach if you eat too fast after starving. Besides, judging by your stuff, I'd say there's not a lot of food left in the world."

"You can say that again," Billy replied. He finished his ramen noodles and regretted it; he hadn't savored them at all, he had barely tasted them. "Sorry about your finger."

"So you did do that? You bit off my finger?"

"Yeah. You were choking me. I was panicking."

"I can't exactly blame you. I was a—a zombie. Do you… know how long?"

"Years," Billy said. "I stopped counting them. Jesus, I didn't know people could turn back. Makes me feel sick to my stomach thinking about things I've done to them."

"I feel sick, too. Physically, I mean. Hey, was there anyone else here? My mother, I can't find her, and her stuff's gone. I remember… I remember biting her."

Billy set his bowl down, staring at the ground, and scratched his face. "If you get bitten, you turn. I'm sorry. There was no one here when I got here, except for you."

"Oh." The woman wiped at her eyes. "Well, thank you, I guess. For biting me. And turning me back."

"That's not what I meant," Billy said. "If a zombie bites *you*, you turn into one of them."

"Yeah, but I *was* one of them. And you weren't, and you bit me, and I turned back."

Billy sat there, his mouth open, his thoughts racing. "Holy shit. I never even thought of that. Nobody ever even thought of that."

"How many people are left, anyway?"

"Your guess is as good as mine. I haven't seen anyone in a few weeks. I try to avoid them. Some aren't friendly, the rest aren't worth the risk."

"What's your name?"

"Billy."

"I'm Lisa."

"It's nice to meet you, Lisa." Tears formed in Billy's eyes. "You wouldn't believe how nice it is to meet you."

"I'm glad I'm not alone, too."

"Lisa, I think I'm going to turn. You bit me, remember?"

"You did turn," Lisa replied. "And I bit you again. Right before you turned, it's what you said to me. 'I bit you back.' I figured it was worth a try. And you attacked me, and I fought you off for a few minutes, and then you just passed out."

A mockingbird cried out somewhere outside. "This changes everything," Billy said. A laugh jumped out of his throat. "This changes absolutely everything, Lisa."

Lisa smiled. "But… What happens now? Where do I go, how do we find everyone and tell them?"

"One person at a time, Billy said. He started to gather his things, and reached for the shoes, but stopped. He realized they were probably Lisa's.

"It's okay," Lisa said. "I have more shoes."

Lisa helped Billy pack up, and between the two of them, the load was much lighter.

Patient One

"What the fuck?" Emily said. "There's two people coming out!" She shifted on her side so she could hand the binoculars to Harrison, lying prone beside her. He took them and gazed through.

Aaron sat in the road a few feet behind them, down the little hill where he wouldn't be seen. The asphalt had dried enough, and his legs were tired.

"So he found someone living in there, no problem," Harrison said. "Plan stays the same. We move in tonight."

"What if it rains tonight?" Aaron said.

"Then we move in in the rain."

They waited an hour for the couple to disappear into the distance, then Harrison gave the order to move.

They had enough water, since they'd been siphoning from the target's rain jug the last few nights. It was heavy, but they didn't have to carry much else. Each of them had a bag, but all three were almost empty. Their sides were weighed down by bats, knives, a nightstick Aaron had grabbed—carefully—off of a zombie who once was an officer of the law, and their prized possession: Harrison's handgun, with ammo for it split between the three of them.

"Got any food?" Emily asked.

"We will tonight," Harrison replied.

"I might faint."

"Suck it up."

Aaron took a candy bar from his bag and handed it to Emily without a word. She took it without a word and ate it without a word. They had to save their strength, and anyway, she would've done the same for him. Harrison would if he had to, but he might never think he had to.

They trudged through the afternoon. At one point they crested a hill when Harrison suddenly dropped to his stomach, and motioned for Emily and Aaron to do the same. After fifteen minutes he got to his knees, then stood and started walking. "They must've stopped for a rest," he said. "Almost came up on them."

"They'll turn in soon," Emily said.

"Sky's gray," Aaron added. "Might rain again tonight."

"Then they won't hear us break in," Harrison replied.

From then on he walked with the binoculars in his hand, looking through them frequently. Finally he stopped walking, headed off the street and across a yard, and hunkered down beside a house. Emily and Aaron followed, and Aaron didn't so much crouch as collapse.

"They're on the other side of the street," Harrison said. "Three houses down. The blue house."

"How long do we wait?" Emily asked.

"I want them to feel comfortable. We can wait for dark, or the rain. Whichever comes first."

The darkness threatened to come first, but as the sky was a dark blue, the rain beat it to the punch, a few drops falling at first, then a sudden downpour.

Harrison almost had to shout, "Let's move."

Quietly, cautiously, they checked all of the doors and windows, but the target had locked them, as he had all the nights before. He was thorough.

"Should've gone in when he broke that window," Emily said.

"I told you, we needed more info," Harrison replied. "Quiet down."

They rounded the side of the house, hopped the waist-high chain link fence, and came upon the back door again. Harrison stared through the glass, looking for light, and when his eyes adjusted, he saw a faint glow coming from the living room, around a corner from the dining room the back door opened on. "Aaron, you're up."

Aaron took his tool kit from his bag and set to work on the lock. It was a simple one, like most of the locks in quiet suburbs tended to be. He pressed his ear to the metal, listened over the rain, tuned it out. He was good at that; tuning things out, paying attention to one thing. It was the only reason he had made it this far at all. With a few minutes of tinkering, something inside the door clicked. Aaron guided the lock out of place, careful not to let it squeak or click,, and then tried the door. It slid open a crack.

"Go time," Harrison said. He drew his handgun from its holster and shoved the back door open. Emily and Aaron followed him in, and Aaron closed the door behind him.

The door was loud enough when it opened, and the targets were already on their way into the dining room. Harrison waited at the entryway with his back to the wall, Emily hunched behind him, and Aaron stayed where he was by the back door. The young man and woman rushed into the dining room, the man wielding a crowbar.

"Hi!" Aaron said, and Harrison clocked the young man in the back of the head, then yanked the crowbar from his hands as soon as he hit the ground. The young woman screamed, but Emily grabbed her from behind and cupped a hand over her mouth.

"Quiet," Harrison said. "No one but the zombies can hear you anyway."

"What the fuck?" the man on the ground moaned. He tried to get up, but Harrison aimed the gun at his head.

"Don't move. We don't want to hurt you, but we will if we have to, believe me."

Painful memories flashed through Aaron's mind. He passed the group and entered the living room, then looked around. A fire was going, a pot of ramen noodles was cooking on it, and several blankets had been placed on two couches sitting across from each other.

"Where's the bag?" Aaron asked. Distant thunder replied.

"My friend asked you a question," Harrison said to the young man. Aaron joined the others in the kitchen. The woman sobbed under Emily's hand, now and then struggling to get free, but Emily held her tight. Both the woman's hands were raised to Emily's arm, and Aaron noticed she was missing a finger. It looked recent. A scar on her arm looked almost like teeth marks, but it was ancient.

"What bag?" the target said.

"The big one you're always lugging around. The one you keep your food and supplies in."

"I don't know what—"

Harrison holstered his gun and drew his baseball bat. He raised it high, and the target put up a hand to block it. "Wait! It's in the hall, by the front door!"

Harrison turned to Aaron, then jerked his head to the side. Aaron went to the front of the house and found the bag. He tried to lift it, almost fell over, and chose to drag it instead. He brought it into the living room, near the fire.

"Move her in there," Harrison said. Emily jerked the young woman into the living room, then threw her to the ground beside the couch. The woman gasped for air.

"Don't fucking move," Emily said.

Harrison drew his gun and put his bat away, then knelt the male target down by the bag. "Open it," he said.

The target opened the bag's pockets and compartments, one by one. Harrison kneeled before him and looked into his eyes. "This thing booby-trapped?" The target shook his head. "I go digging through here, is anything going to pop out at me?" He shook it again. "No?"

"No," the target said.

Harrison smiled. "See? That's all I wanted to know." He started digging through the bag, pulling out a few cans of food, more packets of ramen noodles, and some granola bars. He tossed one of these to Emily, and another to Aaron. Aaron opened his and saw motion; some kind of bug larvae was wiggling around in the spaces between granola grains.

"Blech!" Emily spat a mouthful of granola bar onto the floor. "It's rotten."

"It's not rotten," the target said. "They're harmless."

"You eat this shit?" Harrison asked. The target nodded. He turned to the young woman. "You too? When you got cans of beans and shit?"

The woman opened her mouth, then leaned forward and threw up on the carpet. Aaron moved at the last second to avoid being hit in the crossfire.

"Sure it's not rotten?" Emily asked.

"She hasn't been feeling well," the target said. His eyes lit up, he straightened and opened his mouth, but then he closed it and slumped back down.

Harrison closed his eyes and dug into his granola bar. Aaron flicked a few larvae from his own one by one, then ate it without looking at it. Emily didn't seem bothered at all anymore, downing the bar in three bites.

"There any more food in here?" Harrison asked, gesturing widely at the house. "Any you were planning on taking in the morning?"

"It's all in the bag," the target replied.

"So if I go searching, I'm not going to find anything?"

"No."

"Don't lie to me, now. If I look around and I find any food, I'm going to have to hurt you."

"You don't have to do anything," the target blurted. "Any of it. Everything's going to be okay, we—"

"Spare me," Harrison said. "We're not bad people, we're just hungry, same as you."

"I don't take food from people."

"Yeah, well, if you were smart you would." Harrison left the room, and they heard cabinets and cupboards slamming open and dishes clattering to the floor. The targets winced with every loud crash and bang, until the young woman fainted.

Emily laughed. "Shit, no need to get so worked up. We're not lying, we don't want to hurt you, we just want your stuff. You can even keep your rain thing."

"I don't like this," Aaron said. "Something feels weird."

"God damn it, Aaron, not this again. We've been over it so many times—"

"No, not that," Aaron said. "Something's not right. I think these two are hiding something."

"We're not hiding anything," the target said.

"You know what Harrison will do if he hears you talking like that?" Emily said.

"Yeah. I do. So don't tell him. Let's just get this over with, okay?"

Harrison emerged from the kitchen and headed up the stairs. They listened to him walking around for a while, then he came back down.

"Good news for you, you were telling the truth. I hate it when people lie."

"Just take it and go," the target said.

"Don't think so. It's raining, we're not going anywhere tonight. You can, though."

"You can't be serious," the target said. "It's storming, my bag weighs—"

"Have you not been paying attention?" Harrison said. "You're not taking your bag. It's not your bag anymore. You can keep the water jug only because we don't need it. You and your friend are gonna go, and you're going to be thankful we're letting you keep your clothes."

"Come on, Harrison," Aaron said. "We can take what we have and go."

"Don't 'come on' me, Aaron. They're leaving." Harrison kicked the target's bag, and it toppled over with a loud thump. "And next time, try carrying a lighter load. Jesus, you even use half this stuff?"

"I use all of it—"

"It was a rhetorical question, jackass," Emily said, and then she screamed. Harrison stood up, Aaron reached for his nightstick.

Emily looked down, and everyone followed her gaze. The young woman had woken up and was biting into Emily's ankle.

"Fuck! Let go of me!" Emily jammed her knife into the girl's shoulder. She looked up, her eyes glazed, and moaned.

"Jesus, she's one of them!" Harrison shouted. He raised his gun, but the target tackled him. The gun discharged, a puff of ceiling debris rained into the room, and the two of them hit the ground.

Emily freed her leg and then raised the knife.

"Wait!" the target screamed. "She's not a zombie!"

"She sure fucking looks like one," Emily said, and brought the knife down. Aaron tackled her, and they hit the ground a few feet from the zombie, who started crawling toward them.

"Aaron, what the fuck are you doing?"

"Hear him out," Aaron said.

The target was still wrestling with Harrison over the gun. "Fuck this, Emily said, and tried to stand up, but Aaron pinned her down. "Aaron, get off!"

Harrison yanked the gun from the target, shoved his way to his feet, then kicked the target in the face, sending him sprawling toward the fireplace. Harrison aimed the gun at his head.

"Harrison, don't!" Aaron shouted.

"Asshole," Harrison said, but before he pulled the trigger the target swung the pot of ramen noodles. Harrison screamed and grabbed his face as boiling water splashed across it. Aaron helped Emily up and away from the zombie.

Harrison rolled on the ground, covering his face with both hands. The target picked up the gun and trained it on him.

"No one move," he said, but he looked more afraid than any of them.

"You're dead," Harrison said.

"Harrison, shut the fuck up," Emily replied, "he has your gun." She and Aaron backed farther away from the zombie, which still hadn't thought to get to its feet, instead crawling around the living room. "You want to take care of this zombie?"

"He will," Aaron said. "He has a cure."

Even Harrison looked surprised.

"What the fuck are you talking about?" Emily asked.

"He's right," the target said. "I found this woman in a closet the other day. She bit me, and while we were wrestling, I bit her back. And then I turned, but so did she. I mean, she turned *back*. And then she bit me, and *I* turned back. But I guess that infected her again."

"You're telling me biting zombies makes them human again?"

"Yeah."

"Bullshit," Harrison moaned. "It's all bullshit."

"I'll show you," the target said. He crept up behind the zombie, who was slowly making her way toward Aaron and Emily, and raised one leg of her jeans. The target bit down on her ankle, hard enough to break the skin. "Now help me tie her up."

Aaron joined the target, and after a second, Emily did as well.

"You guys are seriously buying into this shit?" Harrison said. The target kept most of his attention on Harrison while the three of them tied the zombie's arms behind her back and put her on the couch. She wriggled and rotated her head around, but otherwise didn't move.

"How long do we wait?" Emily asked.

"It varies, same as when they bite us." The target reached into his backpack and brought something out, and Emily raised her knife in defense, but he was only offering her a roll of gauze. "For your leg. Oh, and you'll probably turn before she turns back."

Emily looked down at the bite wound in her leg, and tears appeared in her eyes.

"It'll be all right," Aaron said. "You'll turn back."

"How can you know? How can you believe this guy?"

"Look at her arm. Something bit her years ago. And we watched him go in that house alone and come out with a girl who looks like she hasn't eaten in a century. And she was sick when we found her, and then she turned even though we've been watching since they left and we know nothing bit her. His story adds up, Em."

Harrison was sitting a few feet from the fireplace, facing into the corner. He hadn't moved much since being burned, and hadn't said anything.

"I promise," the target said.

"Shut the fuck up," Emily said. She wiped her eyes.

Aaron grabbed her by the shoulders. "Hey, it's okay. If you turn, I'll bite you, and you'll come back."

"So what if he's telling the truth? Then you'll turn."

"And you can bite me if I do. We'll be okay."

"We'll take care of each other," Harrison said. He stood up and faced them. The skin of his cheeks and nose was red. "Just like we always have." He leaned over and picked up the pot, and the target raised the gun at him. Harrison offered the pot to him. "Come on, man. If we're going to be waiting a few hours, you might as well make us all dinner."

Aaron finished his bowl quickly, nut Emily savored every bite. When they were finished they sat around the living room. The target stoked the fire from time to time.

"She hasn't moved," Harrison said. "The zombie." He sounded almost hopeful.

"Might be sleeping," Emily said.

"She's turning back," the target replied.

The storm raged outside. Another hour crept by. Then the person on the couch moaned, turned over, and said, "What happened."

"Son of a bitch," Harrison said. "It actually worked."

"I told you." The target untied the young woman and helped her up. She nearly jumped when she saw Aaron, then she saw the gun in her friend's hand and sighed.

"All right," Emily said. "Tie me up now, I'll take a little nap, and then I'll wake up a regular human being?"

"Yeah," the target said. "As long as someone bites you."

"I'll do it," Harrison said. "Always wondered what it was like to be one of them."

Emily took most of the night to turn. When they were sure she was a zombie, Harrison dug his teeth into her arm.

"Harder," the target said. "You have to break the skin."

He did so, and then they waited.

It stopped raining shortly before the sun came up. No one slept, until Harrison nodded off. They tied him up, and when he opened his eyes, he was a zombie.

Emily came to soon after. She stared up at Aaron standing over her, then sat up.

"It worked?" she said.

"It worked," Aaron replied.

"Harrison?"

"He turned before you turned back."

The male target headed toward them. Emily instinctively reached for her knife, but he offered her his hand. "I'm Billy."

Emily shook it. "Emily."

"I'm Aaron."

"Lisa."

"Well, guys," Aaron said, "I suggest you get your things and get out of here. Far away. We'll wait a while before we bring Harrison back, in case he holds a grudge. He probably wouldn't want me to give you your stuff back."

"Thanks," Billy said.

Emily and Aaron helped Billy and Lisa pack their things, and then they left. A few hours later, Aaron bit into Harrison. He turned back by mid-afternoon, and sat up against the arm of the couch, staring at the ground for a while. "They gone?" he eventually asked.

"Yeah," Aaron said.

"You give them their stuff?"

"Yeah."

Harrison nodded. "I think that guy was right. Everything's going to be okay."

"Yeah," Aaron said, even though he felt a little woozy.

When the three of them left the house early the next morning, they left most of their weapons behind.

The Dead Don't Care

I remember the first time I was bitten. You don't really forget something like that, it has a tendency to stick with you, through thick and thin. You don't so much remember it while you're under, though. Being under is like being on autopilot. You just do things; you wander around and you stick with a horde and you eat. Oh, do you eat.

Now I haven't eaten in days. Not much, at least. Yesterday I found a picked-apart cat in the road and I skinned off whatever parts were untouched, I burned them, and I ate them. There's a grocery store nearby; it's full of people who are under, so there might still be some food in there. I'm going to have to make a run, sneak around and see what I can find.

When you're under though, you feast. Food aplenty, walking the streets and living in pockets of civilization, if you can call it that.

The first one to bite me was my neighbor. I heard screams coming from next door, and being the remotely decent human being I was, I rushed over there, my phone in hand, ready to dial 9-1-1. I saw my neighbor Belinda running down the street in the other direction, blood pouring down her pink robe. Her husband Peter came shambling out the door a few seconds later, and when I said his name, he turned to me with a look more intense than anything I'd ever seen. It wasn't anger or hate in his eyes, it was just hunger.

Peter jumped on me, and I put an arm up to block him. He bit into it like a leg of chicken. Next thing I knew he was crouched low, both hands holding a chunk of my arm to his mouth, eating like a squirrel. I found my phone a few inches away and dialed the police as I stumbled back to my house and locked the door.

I don't remember if I ever got through to the police. People turn at different rates, you know. Some take hours or days. I only took a few minutes to go under.

Of course, I didn't really think about any of this until much later. Like I said, you're on autopilot. But when you come back up, it all comes back to you, all at once.

I wish it didn't come back at all.

****

I was with a horde for a long time. As best as I can remember, we stuck mostly to the highway at first, but back then people still had cars, and almost all of them got away from us. We started heading through fields and woods, coming upon cities, and for a while things were good there.

I was always hungry. You can't die when you're under, not unless something destroys your brain, but you still get hungry. We found people in the cities, but never quite enough to fill our bellies.

I remember this one time, we got inside a building, a tall one. There was a body propping the door open, and this guy, a tall gentleman with half his skin burned off, he figured out pulling on the door opened it up, and he went in, so we followed. He always seemed to catch on to things before the rest of us, so we always followed him.

The bottom floors were empty. We wandered them for days. Someone ate most of the body holding the door open, so it wasn't open anymore when we came back to it. We didn't actually want out though, not yet. We could hear things moving around in that building. At the time we couldn't figure out where the hell they were coming from, but now it's clear they were above us, sometimes even sneaking by us to get supplies from the lower floors.

We finally caught one of them, a young woman, and that's when we knew we'd struck gold. I actually didn't get a bite myself, I came in too late, too many others were in the hall pushing and shoving toward this poor girl, and there was nothing left when the group cleared. But there were more in there, we knew it.

It was that same half-burned tall man who found the stairs. Don't know how he did it, but he figured out how to open the door. When it comes to zombies, that's a pretty neat trick, and some of them see it a thousand times and never figure out how to do it themselves. Well, he grabbed the handle, leaned downward on it, and fell backward, and the door came open. The door slowly slid shut, but he did it again, and the third or fourth time, another zombie finally went through. The rest of us shuffled along, the door hitting each of us in turn, unable to shut. Beyond it were the stairs, and up we went.

We got to the top and couldn't do much else. Most of us stood around on the stairs, and I remember this red-bearded guy decided it was a good idea to shimmy over the railing. He fell a dozen floors or so to the ground below. Not sure I ever saw him again, I think I would remember the aftermath of that little hop.

The burned man finally squeezed between us, got to the door, and opened it up. Into the hall we went. The looks on the faces of the people inside when they realized we'd figured out where they were hiding… *That* was anger and hatred. They hated that we found them out, that they thought they were safe, safe enough to not even bother blocking the door. Who does that? Always block the door. I mean, why wouldn't you?

I have no doubt that if any of them made it out of lunch hour, they double-block the doors now, wherever they are. But I'm pretty sure no one made it out.

****

I don't really remember how I got back to the streets. I know the half-burned tall man made it too, and we stayed with him. After a while it seemed like the city was empty, and buildings were hard to get into, and most of those were empty as well. We moved on together, our unspoken family, our aimless fellowship. I remember grassy hills, some so steep we couldn't work our legs well enough to walk them, so we just rolled down. Is it wrong of me to think of it as fun in retrospect? It wasn't fun at the time, but I have to believe it was now.

People say we can't be blamed for what we did when we were under. Can't be blamed for catching people, killing people, eating people. Well, color my hands red, I had fun with that horde.

We were walking along railroad tracks one night, in and out of abandoned train cars. This must've been years into my being under, when those above had figured out the trick.

Our horde was smaller those days. I must've gotten separated from the others a little, I had heard some rattling coming from one of the train cars, and I had shambled over to check it out. Guess none of the others heard it.

So I was standing there trying to figure out how to open the car, not really thinking but just staring at the thing like it might pop open all on its own, and then it did. Three men in riot gear hopped out and grabbed my arms. I groaned and I grunted, I gnashed my teeth at them, but one wrapped a cloth under my chin and pulled upward, clamping my mouth shut. Another of them lifted his face mask and bit down on my arm. Then they put this device over my head, like a mask with a cage over the mouth, and they hogtied me. I thrashed and writhed, I tried to open my mouth but couldn't, I tried to free myself, but they tossed me in the back of the train car and closed the door. I groaned and grunted, I waited to see if the half-burned tall man would figure out a way to open the train car and free me, but he never came. I never saw him again.

****

I woke up near a campfire, surrounded by people. People who were above, not under. They gave me clothes and they fed me, they explained everything to me.

Someone somewhere had figured out that biting goes both ways. You get bitten by someone who's under, you go under. You get bitten by someone who's above, and you come back up. Unfortunately, the biter gets infected again, and it's only a matter of time before they go back under.

So they have these turning parties. People called turners gear up, they go out in groups, and one by one they try to take back humanity. They bite those who are under to bring them back, do their best to set them up somewhere safe, maybe in a safe zone or a town or a tall building, and then they move on. They have two or three designated biters, people willing to bite the zombies and turn them back, and when they themselves turn, one of the other designated biters bites them, keeping everyone above as much as they can. It's tedious, but, as they explained to me, it's just until some doctor in some lab figures out a *real* cure, and then everyone's biting days are over.

The turning party told me there was a little settlement down the road, and asked if I wanted them to take me there. I told them I'd find it myself, thanked them for what they did, and wished them luck finding the rest of my horde. As I walked down a dirt road that clear night, breathing for the first time in who knew how long, I actually hoped they didn't find them. I mean, that half-burned man, who would want to come back like that? Under, he's a leader. He's the king of his horde, he's the smartest person in the world. Back up here he's just some severely disfigured nobody in a severely disfigured world.

But it was more than that. I think deep down, I knew it even then. I didn't want them found because some part of me felt like changing them back was wrong. They were happy. They felt no pain, they ate most days, they were who they were. They weren't asking anyone to change them.

****

The settlement was a little town tucked away between some steep hills, ones the horde definitely would've had to roll down.

The only easy way into town was a little dirt road, and they had guards watching it at all times. They checked me for bites, and I told them I'd recently been brought back above. They kept me in a cell a few days to make sure, then set me up in a little house near the hill at the back of town.

They gave me a job as a lumberjack. Me and these two other guys around my age had to make sure everyone had enough wood to keep warm on cold nights, and especially during the winter. There was a lot of work in the winter, but I liked it. It was like being on autopilot again; I'd wake up before the sun, strap on my boots, get my tools, and meet the other two at the edge of town. They always had a thermos of coffee ready for me. We'd head out into the woods, an hour or two to make sure the noise from the falling trees didn't bring zombies toward the town, and then start cutting. Some days were spent just transporting wood we'd cut the days before. It was slow-going, monotonous, and it was good.

I was out cutting wood the third time I got bitten. The youngest of the three of us, a young man named Jim, was helping me saw away at a fallen tree when I saw one of them approaching him from behind. I didn't even have time to think of words, I just grabbed Jim and pulled him over the tree, away from the zombie. He fell over the trunk but the person who was under got hold of my arm and bit in.

Trevor, the other worker, clocked it in the head with his axe. I tried to tell him not to kill it, but he didn't listen. By then a small horde was upon us, and Jim helped me to my feet, and we took off through the woods. We came to a little clearing near the road, the people who were under right on our heels.

"We're leading them toward the town!" Trevor said. He tossed me a roll of gauze for my arm. I tossed it back.

"We just had a turning party pass through two days ago," I said. "You two head back toward town. I'll lead the horde their way."

"You'll turn," Jim said.

"I'll try my best to catch up with the turners. If I don't make it, I don't make it. They'll find me eventually."

I didn't give them a chance to argue, I just took off, more toward the horde than not, making as much noise as I could. I started away from the town, and the horde followed. I do hope Jim and Trevor made it back. I'm sure they did; the horde following me looked the same size. By the next afternoon, I was one of them.

****

I'll get back to my story in a minute. Remember that grocery store nearby? I checked it out. Found some food inside. Most of it rotten, but I got out of there with a box of cereal and two cans of corn. It'll do.

I spent some time with the new horde, a much smaller one. This time I was the head honcho. I remembered how to open doors, so they followed me. We never found that little settlement; as far as I know now, it's still there. We wandered the woods and the occasional homes or little stores until the forest cleared into fields, then we came upon a farm. The residents were smart enough to lock the doors, but apparently not enough to cover the windows. A chunky man in our horde silently volunteered to dive face-first through the glass, and the rest of us followed him in.

The farmer had a big family, but most of them got away. We did manage to pick off a young man who decided to play hero to impress his girlfriend. We got his girlfriend, too, because she didn't appreciate his sacrifice enough to use it to escape. The rest of the family made off in a truck and two cars, and for a while my horde followed the dust they left behind. Once it was gone we stayed on that dirt road, and it brought us into a town.

The town was mostly abandoned, but there were a few houses and shops still occupied. We ate again that day, but by the next the town's population was a solid zero. They had wised up and moved on, and they were so much faster than us. God, it's so frustrating how slow you are when you're under.

Some of the others lingered in that town, but most of us pressed on. My horde was down to a little over half a dozen, and now and then someone came or went. We traveled from town to town, through rain and even snow, not feeling wet or cold, only hungry.

Somewhere along the way, we ended up on a coast. Thankfully, we never tried braving the ocean to see what was on the other side. Instead we wandered up and down the coast, sometimes catching seagulls or crabs, rarely eating.

Another turning party laid a trap for us. They dug a deep hole in the ground just off the beach, parked a crane next to it, and hung a net full of people over the hole. We were so stupid, they didn't even need to cover the hole. Our eyes never left the people in the net, writhing and shouting at us. We just walked right into the hole, got up and dusted ourselves off, and reached up at the net, useless as it was.

They would dangle food over the edge of the hole, and when we reached up they would choose someone and yank them up out of the trap, cover their head with those anti-bite masks, bite them, and put them in a cage. One by one I watched my horde dwindle. That was my fourth time being bitten, my second time waking up in a cage, my second time remembering everything.

I must've cried for days, thinking about that farmer's daughter, her boyfriend sacrificing himself for her. Those people in those towns, on the roads; I could almost feel them in my stomach, still being digested.

They offered to escort me to a nearby town. I told them I'd find it on my own, but I wanted nothing to do with it. I decided I'd rather wander this wasteland alone.

****

So that brings us here. I've been at it for weeks, I ate off a dead cat yesterday, I broke into a grocery store and grabbed a box of cereal and two cans of corn. I already ate it all; I just wanted to remember what it's like to taste, one last time.

One of them bit me. I'm trying to be as honest as I can here, so I guess I should come clean and say I let him. Honestly, that's probably why I went in there at all.

I just can't do it anymore. I'm tired of waking up, remembering the things I did while I was under. Truth be told, I was tired of it all even before all this, before all of the bites, what we had back then. But the dead? The dead don't care. When you're under, there is no memory, no farmer's daughters and savior boyfriends, no half-burned tall men waking up to a world that will never accept them, nobody whispering behind your back about the things you did when you were a zombie. There's just you and your food. There's comfort in being on autopilot.

If they bring me back up here again, I'll probably end it. I should end it now; I'm not proud of what I'm going to do when I go under. I can only look forward to falling asleep, knowing that pretty soon, I won't care. There's a town nearby, and I know how to open doors.

Normbies!

The After Life Part I: The Slums of Breathaven

The air smelled like decay, but it was almost an improvement. The occasional waft of fresh air made it worth it for sure. Brook sat with her hands folded behind her head against the tire of a car, watching the sky lighten. Jon was on his knees, his elbows propped on the hood of the car, binoculars to his face.

"Better get moving soon," Brook said.

"Just a minute," Jon replied.

"He's not here." Brook rolled onto her knees beside him. Jon glanced from the binoculars to the dirty little photograph, then through the lenses again.

"Well, there's still the store," he said.

"Exactly. We should head inside and get supplies."

Jon stared through the binoculars for a minute and then put them away, sighing. "All right. You ready?"

Brook stood up. "I've been ready for hours."

They jogged across the parking lot. A zombie dove for Jon, and he leapt to the side, letting it fall on its face. The next one lunged, and he caught it between the teeth with a pipe, then shoved it away. Brook didn't let the third zombie get that close; she shoulder-charged it from behind, sending it flailing its arms as it tumbled forward to the asphalt. A few minutes later they were inside the store. Brook grabbed a row of stacked-together shopping carts and pushed it in front of the door.

Jon lifted the belly of his shirt to wipe his forehead. "It was easier when we could just kill them." Brook laughed, and he looked at her. "What?"

"A lot of people throughout history have probably said those exact words. They probably weren't very good people.."

"Not a good time for philosophy," Jon said. "You hear anything?"

A zombie had started pawing at the front window of the store, apparently unaware of the front door, or unable to pull it open. Other than that the morning was quiet.

"This place really empty?" Brook asked.

"Does anything ever go as planned?" Jon said. "Keep your eyes open."

They walked the aisles looking for any food that hadn't been looted or gone bad. "Jackpot," Brook said, and shoved several bottles of popcorn kernels from the shelf into her bag.

Jon was a few aisles over. "Need a hat?" he said.

"What kind?"

"Beanies, mostly."

Brook shrugged. "Grab them. They'll come in handy when it gets cold."

She heard shuffling as Jon stuffed the beanies into his sack. Brook pressed on, glancing at the shelves. Most were empty, some had cut-open boxes that once contained snack cakes or packages of bubble gum, all were barren now.

"Found some butter for your popcorn," Jon said.

"Fuck you," Brook replied.

"Next best thing then. Catch!"

He tossed something and Brook dropped her bag and caught it. It was a small shaker of salt.

"You're the best! I can't believe nobody took this!"

"It was under the shelf. You have to think outside the box, Brook."

Brook got down on her stomach and turned on her flashlight. She shined the beam under the shelves but found only discarded wrappers, a few receipts, and some chewed-up gum.

"Story of my life," she said.

"What's that?"

"Talking to myself. We should probably head back."

"Nobody is going to notice two normbies missing, and if they do, they won't give two shits."

"You seen A.J. recently?"

"No," Jon said.

"That's because they caught him sneaking back in three days ago. He's been in confinement ever since. I heard they beat him up first."

"Shit. Well, he'll be out as soon as they need the space for some drunk asshole from uptown."

"Or until they get tired of his mouth," Brook said. Jon laughed.

"Yeah, I imagine that'll come first."

They grabbed a few reusable cups and accompanying lids, all of the napkins remaining from their holders, and the only non-rusted pair of tongs from the hot dog machine, then headed for the door.

"Damn it," Jon said. "He made friends."

Three zombies were at the door, pressing against it. One of them had his cheek squished against the glass, wiping the dirt around as his jaw moved up and down.

"Let's try the back," Brook said.

On the far side of the store they came upon a gray door that read "Em oyees Only." Behind it was a cramped little room with a few lockers, a round picnic table and chairs, and a back door beneath a long-dead neon EXIT sign..

Brook opened the back door and a distant echo of panic that an emergency alarm would ring out flared up and then died. She stepped through the door, and a zombie pounced on her from the side. Brook shouted as she fell against the open door, the zombie shoving against her.

"Brook!" Jon shouted. He ran across the break room, but tripped on the leg of one of the chairs.

The zombie pushed its face past Brooks hands. She caught it again, stopping its teeth a centimeter from her face. It pushed through again, and she barely caught it. When it dove a third time, Brook used the half-second it was out of her hands to grab her knife and jam it into the side of the zombie's head. Blood splattered across her face, the zombie went limp and rested its head on her chest like a lover, and Brook screamed.

Jon shoved the zombie's body away and helped Brook up. He pushed and shoved at her, across the back lot of the store, talking about how they had to get away before the zombies came around from the front. Brook's ears were ringing, and suddenly she was stopped with Jon holding her shoulders and looking into her eyes.

"Brook, can you hear me?" Jon was saying. Brook nodded. "Did any blood get in your eyes?"

The idea made her blink. She thought about it, then shook her head. Jon wiped the blood from her forehead and cheeks, then wrapped his arms around her.

"I killed him," Brook said. "We could've helped him."

"Don't start that, it was self-defense."

"Even if he bit me, someone back in town would've turned me back."

"Not if he bit to kill. And they'd put you in confinement for a year if you came back bitten." Brook wiped at her eyes, then hugged Jon back. "Come on," he said. "Let's just get back home."

****

They could see Breathaven from a mile away. Once a small town in the middle of nowhere, now probably the last human settlement in the world. It was surrounded almost completely by rivers and streams, which had been filled with all manner of garbage from the old world: shopping carts, dumpsters, tires, even whole cars. Any zombies that wandered near would get lost in the trash. The only path into town not cut off by water was barricaded end to end and guarded at all times .

Brook and Jon didn't take this path. They went around the town, almost as far from the main gate as possible, where a small hop onto an overturned bus led most of the way across the river of trash. From there they had a series of boards and metal sheets to get them the rest of the way across, and these they would drag onto land and hide when they got back on the other side, both to keep anyone from finding out they had left, and to keep other normbies from wandering into the wilderlands.

It wasn't even noon yet, but Brook felt tired. She barely made the hop onto the bus, and she was panting as they finished hiding their makeshift bridges. When they were done they slipped into the slums of Breathaven.

"No matter how many times we do this, I never get used to the smell," Jon said. "Puts the 'breath' in 'Breathaven', doesn't it?"

Brook stared at the walls as they walked. Some were run-down, most were dirty or painted on. Painting was one of the only ways to pass the time, so most people did it. There was an unspoken language among the citizens, written on the walls. It told stories of epic battles and human history, it showed games played back and forth over months and under layers of acrylic.

At the end of an alley a young boy was painting on the wall. He kneeled, picked up a shard of glass, and cut his palm. His blood became his paint, and he went on with his drawing.

"Ed, that you?" Jon said. The boy looked down the alley at them.

"Yeah. That her blood?"

"No."

"She bit?"

"No. Mind your own business, Ed. Anyone come asking for us?"

"No."

"Do you actually know that, or did you get bored and go somewhere else the whole time we were gone?"

"I stayed right here, asshole," Ed said.

"Good boy." Jon handed Ed a handful of sunflower seeds. Ed wiped his hands on his jeans as fast as he could, took the seeds, and scurried into the streets of Breathaven.

Jon turned to Brook. "You all right, Brook?"

"Yeah," she said. "I'm okay."

Jon smiled. "Good. Let's go."

They left the alley and took a right. Smashed windows and burned-out houses stared at them as they walked the street. There were no sidewalks in some places, and where there were they were cracked or warped, some with weeds growing up between the cracks or gaps.

A laugh poured out of a dead-end alley ahead. They came to it, and an old woman sitting cross-legged on the ground stared up at them, already lifting her trembling hands.

"Brook, Jonathan, tell me you've brought us something. Help me rest easy tonight."

The people in the dead-end lot had quieted down, all staring at the exchange. They sat in a ring around a fire that had been lit inside a tire. Brook kneeled before the woman so she didn't have to reach up and took a bottle of popcorn kernels from her bag.

"For you and your family," she said, and handed the woman the bottle. The woman cradled it like a child.

"Bless you two," the woman said. Some of the crowd by the fire was waving and shouting their thanks. "If it weren't for you lot, we'd all starve."

"I don't know about all that," Jon said. "Anyone got an ash tray?"

Someone near the fire walked across the lot and handed him the bottom fourth of a soda can, all wrinkled and stained. Jon used his shirt to wipe out most of the ashes, then handed it down to Brook. She gave it a second dusting, then sprinkled a pile of salt into it before handing it back to the man. "To give it some flavor," she said.

"Thanks," the man replied.

"We should call you the Angels of Breathaven," the old woman said.

"Just call us your neighbors," Brook replied. "Anyone in town could do what we do."

"But you actually do it," the woman said. She took Brook's hands, squeezed them softly, and then let go. "Have you seen my grandson?"

"A.J.'s in confinement," Brook said. "Don't worry, he's been in there a few days. They're bound to let him out soon."

"How could they do that?" the woman asked. "He's such a good boy."

"He'll be back out here in no time. Tell you what, we'll give him a few weeks off scouting duty, let him spend some time with the family."

"That would be wonderful."

"We'd better get going," Jon said. "We'll see you next time." The woman waved a trembling hand as they continued down the street. They wove through the slums for a while, then Jon said, "You're being too quiet. It's worrying me."

"Sorry," Brook said. She kept seeing that zombie's eyes whenever she closed hers, and it hurt. "Hey, you bang Julia yet?"

"She wants to wait until we're married," Jon replied. He shrugged. "Never a good idea if you ask me, but there's nobody else in this shithole I'd want to be with, so I'll wait."

"So just get married."

"Humans and normbies can't get married. How do you not know that?"

Brook's face felt hot. "Sorry, Jon, I wasn't thinking. Guess I don't think about that kind of stuff much. And I don't know a lot of humans."

"She actually offered to run off and get bitten for me. Make it look like an accident, come back so they'd turn her back, and then marry me and come live downtown."

"Tell me you won't let her do that."

"Of course not," Jon said. "I love her to death for even suggesting it, but I'd never ask her to come to—this." He waved at the dilapidated corpse of a city surrounding them. "Anyway, if we get married, it'll be because we fought for the right to do so. They can't hold us down forever."

"Yeah."

"What about you?"

"I'm sorry?"

Jon stopped walking. "You seeing anyone?"

"Oh. Like I said, I don't think about that stuff very often."

"Brook, you can't be married to your scouting missions. Sure, it's fun now, but at some point you're going to have to retire. Hopefully we'll have de-segregated by then, but either way it might be too late to look. You shouldn't close yourself off now, you're in the prime of your life."

Brook half-grinned. "I am? I feel so dead."

"That's just because you're living in the shadow of the man's thumb. Don't let it keep you down. There's us."

Jon came upon a door with a little arrow painted on it, its tail curving into a circle, a symbol that meant safety and equality. He knocked three times. A muffled voice came from inside.

"What's the password?"

"It's Jon and Brook, let us the fuck in."

Metal slid against metal as the door unlocked, and a teenage boy opened it. "That's not the password."

"And yet you opened the door." Jon pushed into the building, and Brook followed him in, but stopped in the door and looked at the doorkeeper. The kid blushed and looked away.

"Hey, you don't have to worry so much about the password," she said. "It's the safety word you have to listen for, because that means we're being coerced."

"Right. Sorry."

"Don't be sorry. You're doing a good job."

"Sorry. Thanks."

Brook smiled at him and headed down the hallway.

They had set up in what used to be a coffeeshop. Several round tables, each with three or four chairs, dotted a main room. All of the electronics and anything remotely useful had been stripped away long ago, and behind the counter was only boxes full of files and papers and things, so that anyone breaking in might think they were just some kind of history club.

A few people were seated at one of the tables, most of them facing away from the entry hall. The one who wasn't stood up so fast his chair almost fell over, and he stared at them even as he turned and headed for the employees-only room.

The other two turned to look at what he'd seen, noticed Brook and Jon, and stood to meet them.

"Xander'll get the others," said a man with graying hair and a beard. "Group meeting."

"Everyone's here?" Jon asked. "Even A.J.?"

The bearded man and the woman he was with looked at each other. "That's what the meeting's for," she said. The door opened and people filed into the room.

The bearded man stood on his chair. "Everyone, take a seat. Quiet, please, we have something everyone needs to hear."

"Get on with it, Earl," someone shouted. It was an older man named Fisk. "I have night duty, I'd like to get some sleep."

"It's A.J.," Earl said. "You all know he got picked up coming in the other night. Well, they beat him and put him in confinement. One of our inside guys was assigned a confinement shift today. He tells me A.J. died last night."

Fisk sat jaw-agape. A few of the others gasped.

"Died?" Jon said. "What—"

"The beating. Best guess is he had internal bleeding. They thought he was complaining just to complain, but he died from his injuries."

"God damn it!" someone said.

"They can't do this to us, this is too far!"

Earl was holding his hands up for quiet. People liked Earl; he had never gone on a scouting mission himself, he was too old for that, but he had a way with people. They listened to him.

"This is a nightmare," Earl said. "In so many ways, for so many people."

"What do we do?" Xander asked.

"We avenge him," someone else said. A few people shouted their agreement, but Earl held up his hands and calmed them.

"We stick to the plan, for now. I'll come up with something, don't worry. We have to remember why we do this. Our goal is to take the uptowners off of their pedestal, not put ourselves in their place. They've forgotten we're people. Our job is to remind them."

"That's your plan?" Fisk shouted. "Do nothing?"

"No," Earl said. "You're not listening."

"They treat us like shit! They treat us like it's our fault we got bit, like it's our fault we came back! We didn't come back any different, but they treat us like rats! And you want to just sit there while they kill us off!"

"No, I don't! I need time to come up with a plan. In the meantime, we stay the course. There will be no acts of retribution against the uptowners. We don't even know who killed A.J., we're not going to take our anger out on all of them as a whole. That's the entire problem in the first place."

"They're all the same!"

"They're not all the same," Jon said. "My fiancé is an uptowner. Hell, we've got men on the inside, or else we wouldn't be here right now at all."

"He's right," Xander said. "We have to let cooler heads prevail."

"Oh, fuck off." Fisk stood up so hard he knocked the table over, then headed for the doorway. Someone stepped in to stop him, but Earl shook his head.

"Let him go. He's upset, and he has every right to be."

The crowd started to disperse. Earl pulled Brook and Jon aside, then waited for the room to clear.

"Boils my blood just thinking about it," Jon said.

"Tell me you two have some good news."

"We didn't find him out there," Brook said.

Earl shook his head. "Shit."

"Got a plan?"

"We have to find him. It's our best shot. The memorial speech is coming up, we have to hope Warner gives us some idea where he is."

"That's bad news," Jon said. "The memorial is sure to rile people up even more."

"We'll just have to convince them not to do anything stupid," Brook replied. "That's one of the only days they let us uptown. Their guards will be on overdrive, we need to remind everyone to behave."

"We can try," Earl said. "But if Warner doesn't give us something we can use in his memorial speech, I don't think I'll be able to stop some of them from starting a riot."

"That reminds me," Jon said. He took the picture out of his pocket and handed it to Earl, but Earl shook his head.

"Hang on to that. You two are our best scouts. Whether we get a clue or not, I want you two in the wilderlands as soon as the memorial is finished. I need you to find him."

Brook took the picture from Jon. In it was a middle-aged man, Hugh Warner, founder of Breathaven and self-proclaimed leader of the free world, though he rarely mentioned how he was also the leader of the oppression of normbies in its slums. Brook had seen him a few times, but only from the back of the crowd, where they kept the normbies during the memorial speech.

Beside him in the photograph was a teenage boy: Kenneth Warner, his son. He was out in the wilderlands somewhere, and finding him was their best shot at opening Hugh Warner's eyes.

****

The crowd gathered near the gate separating downtown from uptown. There were thirty or forty normbies, everyone present, with one exception: A.J.'s absence was palpable.

Guards stood on top of the barrier, eyeing the crowd. They all had guns, but only one kept his out, his finger on the trigger.

"Look at him," Fisk said. "He's begging us to give him a reason to shoot."

"He's just new," Brook said. "Don't start any trouble today, Fisk. Let's just see how this goes."

Fisk scoffed. "Yeah. We'll see how this goes."

There was a door off to the side of the gate; it opened outward, into downtown. It was so uptowners could come and go freely, or for rare occasions when a normbie was allowed uptown to render some service or perform some duty no one uptown could. The door was always locked and guarded from the inside. Jon was staring at the door.

"You all right?" Brook asked.

"Yeah," Jon said. "Just thinking about the day they let us walk through that door like everyone else."

Brook patted him on the shoulder. "Soon enough. You ready for this?"

"Ready as I can be."

She turned to Fisk. "Fisk?"

"I'm mad as hell."

"I'm mad as hell too, Fisk."

"You don't look it."

"Which is more dangerous, Fisk? The wolf that snarls at you from a distance, or the one that tears your throat out in the night?"

Fisk looked at her. "I'm not going to get anyone killed today, if that's what you're thinking. I'm not like *them*."

"That's all I'm asking, Fisk. Stick to Earl's plan, and soon enough there won't be any *them*. Just *us*, all of us."

Fisk sighed. "Sometimes I think it's too late for that."

"Attention, please," someone said. He stood on top of the gate, in the center. He had an assault rifle, but it was slung over his back. He was Douglas, commander of the guard. "Quiet down everyone? Thanks. You all know how this goes. We're going to open the gate, you're going to head straight down the street, toward Town Square. The crowd's already settled in for the speech. You're to stay in the back, closest to where you arrive. When the speech is over, you turn around and come straight back here for check-in. You know what happens if we catch you skipping check-in?"

"You kill us like you killed A.J.!" Fisk shouted. A dozen people chimed in their agreement.

"I've never killed anyone," Douglas said. "A.J. was a friend of mine. We're dealing with what happened. You going to behave?"

The crowd muttered and moaned, a few people shuffled around.

"This is a holiday. It's a day of remembrance, for people uptown and down. This isn't about you, and it's not about us. It's about the ones we lost, the ones we can't get back. Behave yourselves."

Rusty hinges screamed and thick metal moaned as men pushed the gate open wide, exposing the rest of the street beyond it.

It was night and day. Immediately the graffiti ended, the burned-out houses and broken windows were almost nonexistent on the other side of the wall. Grass was trimmed, broken sidewalks were covered with metal sheets to even them out. There was no trash; all the trash was pushed out into the slums every weekend.

Ahead a crowd three times as large as the normbies was gathered in a little plaza. Some of them turned their heads to look at the approaching mob, most simply ignored them.

To the side of the road an old man sat on his front porch, his rocking chair squeaking as it moved back and forth. He shook his head slowly, scowling. A shotgun rested against the window beside him.

"Not going to watch the speech?" Brook asked him.

"I can hear it from here," he replied. "I like to sit back and make sure none of your kind sneaks into my town."

"One of these days," Brook said, "I'm going to walk through that gate back there, climb your steps, and shake your hand."

The old man grinned. "Don't be so eager to find out what happens when you get up here."

The crowd pressed forward, meeting up with the regular humans. Some of them grimaced, some pushed forward and tried to squeeze away from the normbies.

In the center of a plaza, a small platform had been erected. A man stood on it, next to a gigantic object covered by a sheet in the middle of what was a fountain the last time Brook had been here.

"If I could have quiet," the man on the platform said. No one had been making noise, but he waited for an imaginary lull in the crowd. "Thank you. It's my great pleasure to present to you, on this beautiful day of memorial, the creator and founder of this wonderful town we know as Breathaven, last safe settlement among the wilderlands, final establishment for humanity; our protector and savior, Mr. Hugh Warner."

The man opened his hand to a side as Hugh Warner approached from between two buildings and mounted the steps of the platform. Some of the crowd clapped politely. Warner took a huge bow as he reached the top of the platform, then waited for silence. He didn't wait long.

"Residents of Breathaven," Warner said, "we gather here today, as we do each year, to remember those we lost." He nodded to a group of men on the ground, and they removed the sheet from the object behind Warner. A large sculpture stood, an outer shell of large metal plates welded together, circling a mesh ball in the center, with pipes and spikes jutting out from it.

"Hope no one pokes their eye out," Jon muttered.

"This statue represents a light in the darkness," Warner said. That's what Breathaven is: The last safe place, the only town where people can be people again."

Brook watched Fisk. He clenched his fists, he gritted his teeth.

"I founded Breathaven with the idea that we don't have to leave everything behind. Most of us have lost someone, and I wanted a place where losing our loved ones wasn't the norm. My inspiration was my own son, Kenneth Warner, God rest his soul."

"God rest his soul," the crowd repeated.

"I must've told this story a thousand times. I still see it like it happened yesterday. We were in a shopping mall not far from what's now Breathaven, the day the world changed…"

Brook turned around, searched the crowd for Earl, found him. He was nodding, he was trying not to smile.

"…birthday presents for his mother. I watched in horror as a clerk jumped at him from the dressing room… and then *bit* into him." Warner looked down.

"Stay strong, Mr. Warner!" someone shouted. Warner nodded.

"I had no say in the matter, no power then. I could only watch from across the store as this… *thing* took my only son in its teeth, like a rat. Like vermin."

A few cries of agreement in the crowd.

"We got separated after that. There was so much panic, so many people pushing and shoving. I found that employee, dead from a coat hanger in his eye. I found blood, but I never found my son. I had to go home empty-handed… but you all know how that turned out. My wife was dead when I got home."

"God rest her soul," the crowd said.

"I wanted to give up. I wanted to crawl in a hole somewhere and die. But I didn't. Instead I found this place, mostly empty already, half a ghost town when I got here. I cleared the place out single-handedly, and I made it my home. Over the years, people passed through, and I convinced them to stay. We helped each other build these walls, set up the rules and laws, find peace and happiness here."

"What about happiness for the normbies?" someone screamed. The people at the front of the crowd booed. "We eat dirt, we live in toppled buildings exposed to the rain and snow!"

"We didn't do anything wrong! We're no different from you!"

"You're tainted!" someone shouted back. "You're unnatural!"

"Fuck off!"

"Normbies are no different from us, let them live uptown!"

"Kill the normbies! Kill them before they decide to change back!"

"They'll kill us all!"

The crowd pushed and shouted. Warner cried out for quiet, men with guns approached the circle. Fisk clenched his fist, but Brook took it in her hand. He looked down at her.

"Don't die for this," Brook said. "Not when we finally have what we needed."

A few of the other normbies were staring at Fisk, waiting to see him move. He shook his head and spat on the ground. "Quiet the fuck down everyone," he shouted. "I want to get this over with so I can go to bed."

The crowd slowly stopped shouting, stopped pushing and shoving. When it was as calm as it was going to get, Warner spoke again. "I know things aren't easy for some of you. The simple truth is that we don't know much about this disease, about how it spreads, about whether it'll come back one day. It's necessary to the survival of mankind to maintain these laws we've set, until we have more information that says otherwise."

"When'll that be?" someone asked. "When a scientist pops out of the sky and gives you the all-clear?"

"Yeah!"

"We have a research team —"

"Who's been sitting on their asses for years while we starve and freeze!" someone near Brook shouted.

"Settle down," Brook said, "let's just get this —"

"Fuck you, and fuck Earl. I'm tired of waiting around!"

The man shoved his way through the crowd. The humans parted for him, not wanting him to touch them, one woman threw up when he brushed against her. He headed for the podium. The men with guns took aim, but none had a clear shot.

"Stop!" Warner cried.

"This dies with you!" the man shouted back, and he leapt onto the stage. Warner had already pulled a revolver from his coat and aimed, and a shot rang through the town. Blood splattered the ground of the plaza, and the man's lifeless body fell from the podium.

The gunshot faded into screams. People pushed and shoved, someone elbowed Brook in the eye. She fell backward, but Jon caught her. They struggled to stay on their feet as they pushed through the crowd. On the stage, Warner had dropped to his knees and begun praying for forgiveness; several of his guards had lined up by the platform, guns drawn.

Brook spotted Earl and pointed him out to Jon. He had backed against a wall, and a few of the others were nearby.

"Thank God," Earl said when they arrived. He pulled a map from his pocket and spread it on the ground. It had all kinds of colored spots on it, paintings and markings and little red Xs to show areas no one should bother with. He looked at his color key, then pointed to the map. "Here and here. The only two shopping malls in a fifty-mile radius."

"What if he's left since then?" Xander said. "It's been years."

"We always knew this was a longshot," Earl said. "Brook and Jon, you're taking Xander and Audrey to this one, here. It's farther away. Lyle, Stacy, Nora, and Cody will take this one, here." Earl took a sketched copy of the photograph of Ken Warner and handed it to Nora. "Sorry we don't have a real copy. This is the best we can do."

"We're going now?" Cody asked.

"I'm afraid if we don't do this now, there won't be any normbies to come back to save. Now, remember this picture is old, he'll be a few years older than he was there. He was wearing ripped jeans that day. That's all the info we have."

"Better than nothing," Jon said.

"Marginally," Audrey replied.

"Best wishes, everyone," Earl said, and handed Jon the map. "Let's hope we find him alive. Get going!"

The eight ran down the street, toward the gate. Brook saw the old man from before standing on his porch, holding his shotgun, daring anyone to climb his steps.

A few of the other normbies were running back toward the slums. A gunshot rang out, people screamed. The noise faded as they passed through the gate, where Douglas was shouting "All normbies return to your homes quickly, we don't want to hurt anyone!"

They passed through cracked streets with painted walls, garbage bags littering the curbs. They wove their way through the maze that had been their only home for years, toward the little alley that led to their makeshift bridge. They crossed it and headed through the field, the screams long faded, an occasional gunshot piercing the otherwise still morning. Finally they stopped running and sat to catch their breath among grass reaching higher than their heads.

"So who takes the map?" Nora asked.

"You guys," Brook said. "I know where the mall is. It's where I got bitten."

"Lucky," Lyle said. "Well, for us now, I mean."

"Remember," Jon said, "we need him alive. He's no good to anyone dead. You find him, you try to transport him still turned. If you have bite him, do it, and keep biting each other so we all get back in one piece. If you turn, we can turn you back."

Brook felt a pain in her heart for the man she'd killed on her supply run a few days earlier. She wouldn't make that mistake again; turning wasn't the end of the world.

"All right," Jon said. "Let's hope we find this guy out there."

The group said their goodbyes, then split into two and headed into the wilderlands.

Normbies!

The Journal of Dr. Rory MacKay

or

The Post-Apocalyptic Prometheus

September 1st, 2020?

This is about as legit as it gets.

Let me back up. That date up there is a rough estimate. Most of us stopped counting days a long time ago. Others have kept journals or records and they swear by them, but I've seen three different dates from such people, so to hell with it all, I'm pretty sure it's 2020 and I think it's September-ish, so that's where I'm starting.

I've been set up in a hospital. It's bittersweet; it's a taste of my old life, which isn't something many people get, but my old life wasn't exactly full of joy. You have to detach yourself to tell people they're going to die or tell people's loved ones they didn't make it, but you never detach yourself fully. Then again, after all the shit I've seen the past five or so years, it's probably going to be a lot easier now.

Anyway, I'm with the military. Well, it's not *the* military, but it is a group of former soldiers. They obviously don't have contact with any generals or presidents because those things don't exist anymore, but they have the tools and the weapons and the uniforms, which is to say they have the means, so this is as good as it gets.

Not only do I get to work, I get to be safe. Mostly safe, at least; you're never really safe. They want me to study this… whatever it is. Virus? Bacteria? Disorder? Supernatural event? Let's find out together!

September 3rd, 2020

The boys brought in a truck full of Turned patients. I picked one at random and we strapped her to a table to begin my research.

I started with an autopsy. Well, something like an autopsy. The patient wasn't exactly deceased; not more than the average Turned is, anyway. We rendered her harmless, and I began my work.

My first observation is that they don't appear to feel any pain. I administered no anesthetic of any kind, yet the patient didn't respond to the first incision. She grunted and shifted as they always do, but made no sounds or movements to indicate she was aware of what I was doing, even when I popped her ribcage open.

I started systematic removal of her vital organs. This had zero effect on the patient. No heart, no lungs, no stomach, no liver, no kidneys, no lungs, yet her mouth moved up and down inside that mask, she turned her head side to side, she wriggled her fingers. It's true what everyone says; you have to destroy the brain.

And I mean <u>destroy</u> it! I opened the patient's cranium and tinkered around, careful not to sever the brain. I couldn't elicit any motor response, no matter what I did. Whatever keeps these things moving, it's not biological. Not in any fashion we understand.

I took tissue samples of all of the above and put her back together. More testing is needed, but I'm ~~turning in~~ going to bed.

September 4th, 2020

Microscopic study of the tissues taken from TP-100 (female patient from yesterday) showed nothing. The tissue is dead, the blood is dead, the brain is dead, it's all dead. There are even some signs of decay. The Turned are, for all intents and purposes, deceased. And yet they move. I will find out how.

September 6th, 2020

The afternoon of September 4th, I bit the bullet and had a member of the turning party bite into TP-100. Subject took almost a full day to turn back, and I took skin and blood samples along the way.

Turning back appears to be a systematic process, not all at once. Everything reanimates, starting with the blood, then organ tissue, then skin. The Turned essentially come back to life from the inside out.

Cognitive awareness came last, as appears to be constant in all cases.

TP-100 is a middle-aged woman named Barbara. We're going to nurse her back to health for a few days, then send her on her way.

September 7th, 2020

I interviewed Barbara. She remembers the operation well, but doesn't remember feeling any pain. This is good; I wouldn't exactly feel guilty if she had, but I do rest easier knowing it was painless.

I picked a new patient from the group. TP-101 will continue where we left off with Barbara.

I took blood samples, for all the good they'll do me. Better to have it and not need it, right?

This one will be interesting. TP-101 was a young male, and has received severe trauma to the right arm; we're going to remove it later today. It's why I chose this one.

Checking in again. Removal of TP-101's arm was easy. Subject appeared to feel no pain, as with Barbara. Minimal tools were needed; patient did not bleed during the procedure, delicacy was hardly necessary.

September 10th, 2020

The past few days were hell. I have to remember the *reason* for this, or I won't be able to continue. It's all in the name of science.

We decided to turn TP-101 back. Process took only a few hours. Somewhere along the way, the patient's heart began beating. I had left the amputated arm untreated. I don't know what I expected to happen, but it started bleeding everywhere. I decided to stitch it back up, but the patient regained consciousness first.

The timing couldn't have been worse. There was nobody else around, and I was busy stopping the blood, I couldn't risk administering an anesthetic. I had to sew the patient's arm up with him tied to the gurney, screaming out loud and feeling everything.

His name is Eric. I apologized profusely, and from now on when we turn someone back, I'm keeping at least one soldier handy to assist me.

September 19th, 2020

I told Eric I would make things up to him by giving him a new arm. He doesn't trust me, and I don't exactly blame him, after what happened. I'm doing this for my research as much as for his benefit, but that didn't seem to comfort him much.

I told him the plan: We were going to turn him back into a zombie. That's about as far as I got before he started protesting, but I convinced him to hear me out. (One of the soldiers helped. No, not like that—Ellen, the soldier, didn't lay a finger on him, she's just an intimidating individual.) We turn Eric, I find an arm from our... discard pile, stitch it to him, and bring him back. With luck, the arm takes.

I believe in honesty with my patients. I told him there would be a long road ahead of him, he would have to slowly regain control over his arm (assuming I could successfully attach one), and there was a chance his body might reject the arm. I don't have access to all the necessary drugs, and it could be years before the body rejects the arm anyway, so I told him there was a chance he would have to self-amputate it in a few years if it got too bad.

He refused the operation, of course. The fact that I don't get a choice didn't make it any easier for me to tell him he didn't get one either.

The surgery was a success. We put him under, I attached the arm in what has to be the fastest and easiest reattachment surgery in the history of mankind, and we brought him back up after a few days.

The arm reanimated with him. It was fascinating to see. And something extraordinary happened: it healed almost immediately. Eric won't exactly be playing football anytime soon, but it's as though he's recovering from a cut rather than a full limb reattachment surgery. It's as though the arm always belonged to him. I can't know of course, but based on what I'm seeing, I don't think he'll reject the arm at all.

I can tell Eric hates me, but this morning he thanked me, and it was genuine. He didn't expect it to work. I didn't know what I expected, but it wasn't this. I need to make sure Eric isn't a fluke. I need to test another patient.

September 27th, 2020

I couldn't bring myself to dismember any of the Turned, so I waited for the soldiers to find me a viable candidate. They brought me a Turned with severe leg trauma, said it was crushed under a pallet jack in a warehouse somewhere.

I wanted so badly to use a leg of a different blood type, just to see what would happen, but I'm already treading a fine moral line here. In the end I couldn't pull that trigger. I gave TP-102 a leg replacement, and I hate to pat myself on the back, but I made a damn good fit.

Patient was resurrected yesterday afternoon. A man named Yancey. His recovery is on par with Eric's. It's extraordinary, really. I'll continue to monitor them both.

We sent Barbara on her way a few days ago. I wish her the best out there.

October 5th, 2020

Work has begun on study of the bites themselves. I have three patients, TP-200 through TP-202.

We already knew this event (I can't call it a virus, because it isn't. Look as I might, I don't see anything but living or dead cells under the microscope, and none that aren't supposed to be there) was communicable through blood—get Turned blood in a cut or your eyes, and you turn. The same goes for saliva in a wound, and as we now know, that works backwards, but what about blood?

I volunteered my own for the first experiment. A drop of my blood was placed in TP-200's right eye. Patient took less than a day to turn back.

This is good news, especially for the turning parties. While a bite still works in a pinch, the fact that we can use a blood injection to turn people back—regardless of blood type, it turns out!—means an easier process with much less visible scarring.

The process was replicated in patients TP-201 and TP-202.

I turned all three patients several more times, and it appears as though a full turn must take effect before a new one can, meaning if someone gets bitten by a Turned, and an Unturned bites them before they turn, nothing happens. It doesn't counter-act the bite, and the one who bites them won't be turned (unless they have some kind of open wound in their mouth, anyway). The cycle has to run its course. The same goes for the reversal.

Oh, and repeated turning appears to have no lasting impact on the patients, other than making them loathe me. I recommended all three for placement in the nicest—and farthest—safe zone we know of.

October 9th, 2020

The soldiers brought me a Turned that was hardly more than a head (TP-300). With the brain intact, TP-300 was still active (I don't know that the term "alive" applies here).

It took only a few minutes to un-Turn this one (is it related to body mass? I think not; I've seen fat men turn in hours and children take days, I'm chocking this up to coincidence). The patient died almost immediately, being little more than a head.

I guess my old instincts kicked in, and I tried my hardest to save it. As science and medicine evolve, so do the tools we use to implement them. I immediately injected the patient with a vial of Turned blood. To my surprise, it reanimated as a Turned.

We didn't have any headless corpses in our discard pile, so I stitched together the best thing I could with the best parts I had, attached TP-300, and injected it with Unturned blood. Patient took a few hours to revive. Patient is understandably in great duress, not recognizing any part of her own body. I couldn't get a name out of her. Couldn't get much of anything, really. She hates me, she won't touch any food I give her, she hides under the bed if I so much as approach her room. I have Ellen or one of the other soldiers bring her food and check on her.

October 10th, 2020

TP-300 (I hate that I don't have a real name to call her by) continues to survive. She acts almost feral, but not like the Turned—she's an extremely disturbed human being.

The success of this and the other operations has monumental implications. There's almost no such thing as death anymore, I can bring almost anyone back from anything. I could do a full-body transplant, what they call in science fiction circles a "brain transplant." Anyone can be anyone, look like anything; think of what this would do for the transgender community, for soldiers maimed in war, for burn victims. The best part? No need for matching blood types, no need for anesthetics. ~~Speaking in strictly medical terms, this apocalypse is the best thing to ever happen to mankind.~~

Can you imagine a child who lost their parents reading that last sentence? Jesus Christ.

October 11th, 2020

Despite my efforts, a cure eludes me. Try as I might, I can't replicate these experiments with anything other than blood. Turned vs. Unturned, it doesn't matter. An artificial cure for Turning has to exist, but I'm running out of ideas on where to find it.

For now, we stick to what we have. This system is rudimentary, but it works. Hats off to the turning parties, those people who agree to turn over and over again so strangers can have another chance at life.

October 12th, 2020

Ellen woke me this morning and told me TP-300 had killed herself.

We held a military funeral for her. She was no soldier, but she helped us so much.

I had a bit of an argument with one of the superior officers, Sergeant Kearns. I told him I didn't want to do anything on that scale again. He firmly reminded me that I'm to do whatever they ask of me, or they'll find someone else who will.

October 17th, 2020

They're looking for me now. It all changed so fast. But I couldn't do it, they couldn't make me. She was just a little girl.

I'm in one of the back rooms now, afraid to even scribble in here whenever I hear bootsteps. But I have to write it down or nobody will ever know, they'll make it like it never happened.

I thought about leaving for days, I ran it over and over in my head, not sleeping, sometimes dreaming anyway, having nightmares flash before my eyes. And then what they ~~asked~~ told me to do… No no no.

This is why things got like this in the first place. Of what humanity is, what it does to itself. I know without a doubt now that this is a supernatural event: something that happened, that can be studied, but isn't random. This didn't happen for no reason, the only virus here is us. The only disease is _US_.

I think we all wondered why, even from the beginning. My first thought was overpopulation, the world was taking us out before we took it out, a host rejecting its parasite. But my research proves that wrong. I circumvented death itself, so the reason can't be overpopulation. I alone have done more damage on that front than seven billion procreating human beings in a hundred years. Not bad, for a month and a half of research.

My next thought was war. For once in our history, we couldn't afford to fight each other anymore. But again, my research proves the opposite, doesn't it? From now on we can blow each other's soldiers to bits over and over again, and the only deciding factor will be which country's medics can stitch their soldiers back together faster.

I can only believe that we weren't supposed to learn how this works. This was supposed to end us; it's pure coincidence that we figured out how to circumvent it. That's what a good disease does, it finds a way around the cure.

Call it the Universe or call it Nature or call it God, but this was a last-ditch effort to get rid of us for good, and we bounced back, just like we always do.

That's why I burned it all. Everything in my lab, all of my notes, all of my research. It's why I have to die, and I mean DIE. I don't care who they think they'll find, nobody will ever be able to put this humpty dumpty back together again, I can fucking guarantee them that.

This journal will remain. It'll remind them, it'll tell the world what happened, maybe convince people not to pick up my research, not to follow in my footsteps. I've paved a road that leads straight to hell on earth. Please, for the love of whatever you can bring yourself to believe in, don't follow it.

I'm giving this diary to Ellen. She's already promised to take Gwen, that little girl, out of this nightmare. When I think of that, I come as close as I ever could to having any hope for us. We're not all bad, we never were. There are good people in this world.

I hope what I'm doing makes me one of them. The best thing I can possibly do for the future of mankind is cease to exist, to die unremembered.

Don't make the same mistakes as me. We weren't meant to know everything. We weren't meant to have this power. This was always supposed to be the end of us, so let it be the end.

I don't blame you if you try to survive in this world, but please… please, when you die, do your best to stay dead. It's the only hope we have.

The After Life Part II: Bravery

"All normbies return to your homes quickly," Douglas shouted, "we don't want to hurt anyone!"

He waved his hand as though that would make the crowd move faster. One of his sergeants was running along the gate toward him.

"Douglas, Warner wants you in Town Square! He's in danger!"

"Just keep ushering them along!" Douglas said. The sergeant took his place at the center of the gate, and Douglas headed for Town Square.

He pushed passed normbies and people alike, most of them running the direction opposite him. Ahead he saw a young guard hit a normbie in the face with the butt of his gun. The man hit the ground hard, then put his hands up over his face as the guard turned the gun on him.

"Don't!" Douglas shouted, but the man pulled the trigger. What was a panic turned into chaos. People shoved each other down, guards fought normbies and normbie sympathizers. A few tried for their guns. "Hold your goddamn fire!" Douglas screamed, and most did, but he heard another gunshot ring out.

"Douglas!" Warner screamed. "Get your ass over here!" He was crouched on the ground beside the podium, right in front of his light in the darkness statue, near the normbie he'd shot in the face earlier. He still had his revolver in hand.

"This way, sir," Douglas said. Warner came to his side. A normbie noticed and rushed at them, a beer bottle in hand. "Don't do it—" Douglas punched the man out before he could bring the bottle down at either of them. He turned back to Warner. "Stay right beside me, sir. We've trained for this."

Douglas started through the crowd, between passing rows of people and the occasional normbie. Most of both seemed to be more confused than anything else. Warner stuck right by Douglas's side as he headed for a very specific alley, then to a specific door.

Douglas tapped a musical tap, and the door opened. Douglas shoved Warner inside, then ran back toward the street. A guard was raising his gun, and Douglas charged him, knocking him to the ground, then spun and caught the fist of the normbie who had been about to punch him. He kneed the woman in the gut, winding her, then helped the guard up.

"Guns down, repeat, do not fire!"

"They're attacking us!" the guard replied.

"Unless your life is in immediate danger of ending, do not fire your weapon, or I'll make sure it is, you understand me?"

"Sir!" The guard holstered his gun and drew a baton. Douglas pushed through the throng and grabbed a normbie who was wailing on one of his sergeants, threw the man in the direction of the gate, and gave the guard (who appeared to have been disarmed at some point) his own baton. Douglas moved for the next visible altercation, two normbies beating a guard who was lying on the ground, trying her best to curl up and block the blows.

Douglas sucker punched the first normbie, who fell backward. He grabbed the next by his shoulder and wrist, spun him away, and shoved him as hard as he could. "Go back to your home!" he shouted. The man, on his hands and knees, turned his head toward Douglas.

"Back to the slum? Fuck yourself!"

Douglas kicked the man in the stomach, not hard enough to hurt him, but enough to make him change his mind. The other normbie was creeping up behind him, he could see the shadow. Douglas rounded on him in time to catch a punch to the face, caught the next punch in his hand, and twisted the man's wrist. He fell to one knee, and Douglas let him go. The man backed away, raising his hands.

"Back home! Now!"

Both normbies ran off. A gunshot rang out somewhere, Douglas helped the wounded guard to her feet, and then, with the slamming of a few nearby doors, the remains of the gunshots fading away, and someone crying out in pain, the fight was over.

****

Ashley dropped a manila envelope on Douglas's desk. He was leaning back in his chair, holding an ice pack to his eye.

"Full report, sir," Ashley said. "Three dead: The normbie who rushed Warner, another normbie shot in the head, and a guard beaten with a cement block. Two in critical condition, a human kid who got trampled and a normbie who took a severe beating. Dozens wounded, mostly people complaining that they got pushed too hard, but a few more serious injuries. And we have three normbies in confinement."

"Jesus Christ," Douglas said. "This is all my fault."

Ashley raised an eyebrow. "What, because you were by the main gate when it happened? You couldn't have stopped this, Dan."

"Not what I meant. Never mind."

"Well, if you hadn't stopped those two normbies, I don't know what would have happened to me." She leaned in close. "And anyway, Warner fired the first shot."

"Yeah, well, a normbie rushed him first. Don't let people hear you talking like that. Any word on if Audrey got out?"

"She's not among the dead or confined, I know that much. Hey, Warner wants to see you, by the way."

"Warner's asking for me? And you didn't start with that?"

Ashley shrugged. "He said at your convenience."

"Warner never cares about anyone else's convenience. Start with that next time?"

"Yeah. Sorry."

"It's okay, Ash. Get some rest."

"You too, Dan. As soon as Warner is done with you, I mean."

Ashley left his office. Douglas put the report in a drawer, then left the office and headed down the hall. Ahead he saw two guards standing outside a door, whispering into a little slot in the metal.

"What are you two doing?" Douglas asked. They straightened up right away; one was holding a tray with three plates of food on it.

"Nothing, sir, just feeding the prisoners."

"They're starving us!" someone inside the room shouted. "Said they'd eat our food while we watched!."

Douglas looked the two guards over. "Names?"

"Sir, they killed McKinney! It's not right!"

"Did you see any of these three kill McKinney?"

"No, but—"

"We don't torture prisoners, we definitely don't torture prisoners for things they didn't do. What are your names?"

"Michael Anderson," the other guard said.

"And you?" Douglas said.

"Sir—"

"Your name is 'Sir'? Your superior officer asked you a question. I suggest you answer it."

"Jack Doser."

"Private Anderson, feed the prisoners and then return to your post. Private Doser—"

"I'm a lieutenant, sir."

"You're a private now. Private Doser, find private Louis Leclerc and relieve him of janitorial duties. They're yours for the next two weeks."

"Yes sir," Doser said through gritted teeth. He handed the tray to Anderson and stormed off.

Douglas peered into the confinement room through the slot. "Any of you three know who killed Sergeant McKinney?"

The prisoners were an old man, a young man, and a young woman. They looked at each other. "No sir," the young woman said. Douglas barely heard her; his eyes were on the old man. He was the one who had rushed Warner with a beer bottle. Douglas sighed and turned to Anderson.

"Bring them some coffee and blankets. Make sure they're comfortable tonight."

"Yes sir."

Douglas started down the hall again. At the end of it was a door with an opaque window set in it, and on it were block letters:

Hugh Warner
Founder of Breathaven

Douglas knocked on the door. Warner opened it.

"Ah, Commander Douglas. Come in."

He held the door wide as Douglas entered. Warner took a sturdy padded seat behind a large desk, and motioned for Douglas to sit down in a little wooden chair.

"Sorry I'm late, Mr. Warner. Had some duties to finish up."

"You're not late at all. I just wanted to thank you for saving my life today."

Douglas scratched the back of his neck. "Just doing my job."

"And doing it well," Warner said. "Cohen's been gunning for your position, you know. I even considered giving it to him, but after today I think that's off the table." He opened a drawer and removed a tiny wooden case from it. "That man I killed... It's never easy, is it?"

"No sir."

"I just wish they would listen to me. I wish they could understand."

"If I may speak freely, sir..."

"Do, please," Warner said.

"They don't like being segregated. They get a fifth as much rations as the rest of us, they have stricter rules. They're unhappy."

Warner leaned back in his chair, eyeing Douglas with what could be curiosity or vitriol, maybe some balance of both. "I know.

And it does break my heart, Commander. But it's a necessary evil." Douglas nodded and looked down a little, at Warner's desk. "I can tell you're less certain."

"I understand some of the rules," Douglas said. "We don't know how this thing spreads, if it can come back stronger. I just—"

"Your girlfriend, Audrey Hartwell. She's a normbie." Douglas looked up from the desk. "Surprised? I keep track of these things, as any leader should. She's not one of the three in confinement, is she?"

"No, sir."

Warner's eyes widened, he sat up straight. "The morgue?"

"No sir."

Warner relaxed. "Good, good. You among others have a heightened sense of sympathy toward the normbies. That's normal. I wish more people did."

"Some of our people are just as upset."

"Those are the ones we really need to worry about," Warner said. "The normbies have their place. It's about health and safety, sure, but it's about more. It's about reminding people they could have it so much worse. People... we're funny creatures, aren't we? We have to be above someone else or we're not happy. And it can't be just anyone, like the zombies out there." Warner nodded his head to the left, as though the wilderlands were just beyond his wall. "It has to be someone close by. It has to be the normbies."

Douglas bit his tongue. He could've asked, *What about them? Who are they above?* but he knew better.

Warner leaned forward, took the tiny box, and slid it across the desk toward Douglas. "That's for you."

Douglas opened it and found a medal, a tiny star molded of the goldest-looking scrap metal Warner was able to find.

"Sir, I don't—"

"You do deserve it, Commander Dan Douglas. I, Hugh Warner, hereby award you the Breathaven Medal of Bravery. Not just for what you did for me, but what you do for all of us, every day." Warner stood up and looked at a painting on his wall, a drawing of Breathaven he had commissioned shortly after its founding. "I run this civilization, sure enough. But I couldn't do it without help. From people like you." Warner crossed the room, took the medal, and affixed it to Douglas's overcoat.

Douglas didn't know what else to say, so he said, "Thank you, sir."

"One last thing. How is the investigation into the death of that poor normbie going?"

"Dead ends," Douglas said. "If I find anything, I'll let you know."

Warner nodded. "Do. But be mindful of our resources. We have, as they used to say, bigger fish to fry. You're dismissed."

Douglas left Warner's office and had to struggle not to slam the door. Memories chased him down the hall toward the barracks, memories of a few nights earlier, when they caught that normbie, A.J., sneaking back into town, and it couldn't be just anyone who caught him, no. It had to be Herman Cohen, the meanest son of a bitch on the force. And of course he had to start throwing punches, him and his cheeky-faced lieutenants. Then he challenged Douglas to do something about the problem, to really *do* something, and what could he do? They would all go to Warner with allegations of leaks in the wall and normbies running amok through Breathaven proper, true or not, and Douglas would lose his job, which seemed so much worse at the time, but the moment had caught him, and Douglas threw a punch at A.J. himself, and then another, and then A.J. spat blood, and they brought him to the infirmary, but he never came back out.

Douglas threw open the door of his quarters so hard, the knob punched a hole in the wall. He slammed it shut again, tore the Breathaven Medal of Bravery from his jacket and threw it, and lay face-down on his bed. He screamed into his pillow, screamed as loud as he could knowing no one could hear, and eventually cried himself to sleep.

Shiloh

Wayne Hewitt counted fourteen zombies in the lot, and he only wished there were more.

He stood up behind the car, nocked an arrow and drew, then let loose. By the time the first zombie hit the ground with an arrow through its head, he had let two more go. One missed and hit a zombie through the neck, but the last arrow rammed through another zombie's skull and out its eye, killing it.

The zombie that had been hit in the neck turned slowly toward the source of the impact and spotted Wayne. It groaned and started toward him, alerting the other eleven zombies.

Wayne slung the bow over his shoulder and drew his machete. He met the arrow-necked zombie halfway, and with a heavy swing took off the top of its head. He rammed the machete through the next zombie's face and pulled it out, slinging a trail of blood across the pavement. He jammed the machete up through the next zombie's chin and into its brain. The zombie fell hard, taking the machete with it.

Wayne drew a knife and threw it, and it landed in an approaching zombie's eye. The zombie fell, tripping the one behind it, and when it hit the pavement, Wayne stomped on its head as hard as he could, crushing it like a half-rotten melon.

Halfway there.

Wayne knelt down, and the next zombie rolled over him while he yanked his machete free. He brought it down into the fallen zombie's head, then swung it as he turned, decapitating the next zombie. The one after was upon him before he could recover from the swing, and it caught him by the arm and bit at him. Wayne pulled back and heard a *clat!* as the zombie's teeth clicked together. He head-butted the zombie, and it didn't seem to feel any pain, but the blow pushed it onto its backside. Wayne brought his steel-toed boot into the zombie's jaw, threw his machete at one farther away, then got out his chain.

He started with the zombie he had just kicked, wrapping the chain around its head from jaw to pate, then pulling up as hard as he could. The years of decay had done most of the work for him, and the chain came up like a knife through butter, severing the front of the creature's head from the rest of it.

The next zombie was upon him, and when it lunged Wayne pulled the chain taut, catching it between its jaws. Pulling on both ends of the chain, he shoved the zombie hard, guiding it to the ground, where he stomped its head in.

Wayne let the chain drop with the zombie and slid two knives from their holsters at his sides. The last two zombies came at the same time, and when one lunged, he side-stepped it, catching the zombie with his knife in its eye. He let the knife drop, put both hands on his other knife, and lunged at the final zombie. The knife connected with its forehead, driving deeper as the two of them fell to the asphalt.

Wayne rolled off of the zombie and lay on his back, panting hard. His muscles screamed at him; he wasn't as fit as he was in his football days. Hell, he wasn't even as fit as his early zombie hunting days.

He heard a noise to his left and turned his head. The zombie he had decapitated was still moving, clacking its jaws up and down, unable to do much else. Wayne gathered his knives, machete, chain, and arrows, cleaned them off, then kneeled near the severed head.

"Look at you. Never thought this would happen, did you? Thought this was your world? This is *my* world, you sum'bitch." Wayne stood and started walking away, but stopped. It was hard sometimes to remember that these things were people once, that they didn't ask for this. Whether it was some government experiment gone wrong or God's punishment, Wayne couldn't say. In the end, leaving it to suffer this fate just didn't seem right. Wayne dirtied his machete again putting the disembodied head out of its former owner's misery.

****

He still had plenty of ammo. He didn't use guns often; he had several of them and what once looked like enough ammo for ten zombie apocalypses, but he learned early on that the sound only drew more in. He made sure to tell people that on the few occasions he met strangers out in the world, ones who needed the guns and ammo more than he did. He also made sure to tell them they should've been stockpiling long before day zero. "We knew this was coming," he would say. "We tried to tell people, but they didn't want to hear it." Still, it was the right thing to do, giving them the tools to survive another day. "Last resort only, though. These things will draw every last sucker for miles."

As it got darker, Wayne realized he wasn't going to come upon another town, not tonight. He went off the road a ways and set up a little campfire. He hadn't seen a zombie since the parking lot, and he was pretty sure everyone in these parts knew to leave him alone.

Some bandits tried to take his food once. They thought they got all his weapons from him, but he kept a spring-loaded knife up each sleeve. He got the first bandit in the throat, and even though the guy had Wayne's gun, he was too panicked from the blood to use it. That gave him the jump on the other three. By the time he had practically hacked two of them to bits, the last was throwing down Wayne's shotgun and begging for his life. Wayne left him chained to a streetlight, fired his gun into the air several times, and crept away into the night. The next morning he came back and took plenty of pictures of the scene (including the handful of zombies he finished off) in case the next bandits didn't believe his story. Word must travel fast in bandit circles; no one had tried to rob him since.

He cooked a rabbit he had caught over the campfire, ate a nice dinner, and set to cleaning its pelt. He had a few of them stored up; when it got cold he would use them for warmth.

This is how it should be. This is how it always should've been.

Wayne used some of the old pelts as a pillow (the new one needed to dry), and under the stars, he slept like a baby.

****

Little black dots shimmered on the horizon. Wayne shifted his backpack to keep it from obstructing access to any of his weapons, unbuttoned his holsters, and got his binoculars out.

It was a young couple, walking toward him. Clearly not zombies. Maybe still bandits. He put the binoculars away and kept moving. Soon they noticed him, and Wayne could see them whispering to each other, sizing him up.

Wayne stopped walking a few yards ahead of them and set his backpack down. They stopped as well. "I ain't going to harm you. Not unless you give me a reason to."

"We don't want trouble," the young man said. "We're just passing through."

"Same," Wayne said. "Here. Peace offering." He took out a Ziploc bag with the rest of the rabbit he had cooked the night before and tossed it to the couple. The woman caught it. "Damn fine catch, miss."

"What is it?" the young man asked.

"Rabbit. Caught it and cooked it last night. You're not vegetarians, are you?"

"We were," the woman said, already opening the bag. Her husband seemed wary, but made no move to stop her. "Can't really afford to be, these days."

"No you can't."

"Thanks," the young man said. His wife offered him some of the rabbit, and he devoured it.

"Where you two headed?"

"There's a small town on this road, unless we got lost somewhere. Shiprock."

"Yep, it's there," Wayne said. "Not sure what you want from it, though. Not much there but a parking lot full of dead zombies. Just came from that way."

"There's a reservation nearby. We thought it might be a good place to lie low, not heavily populated, might even have some supplies."

"I wouldn't know anything about that," Wayne said. He picked up his backpack and started toward them. "Nice meeting you folks."

"Thanks again," the woman said. "For the food." Her husband whispered something in her ear, and she nodded. "Hey, have you heard about the cure?"

Wayne stopped walking and almost dropped his backpack. He squinted at the couple. "Beg pardon?"

"There's a cure, it's true," the man said. "Look here." He raised his pant leg to reveal a bite. It was old, mostly healed, but definitely a bite. His wife hugged him.

"They've been biting us and turning us for so long, somebody finally figured out to bite them back. It turns them, too."

"You telling me he got bit, became one of those fuckers, and then you bit him and turned him back?"

The couple's smiles faded. Maybe Wayne sounded angrier than he meant to.

"No," the woman said. "I mean, *I* didn't bite him. Some people saved me, right after he got bit, they're the ones who told us this. I guess they go around biting people who've been bitten and changing them back. Biting someone who's infected changes you, too. But if you've got friends with you, you can just keep changing each other back."

"It sounds like horseshit."

"It's the truth, sir," the man said. "I was only one of them for a few hours. I had locked myself in a store, and my wife brought them back to me and they changed me back. This was maybe two weeks ago."

"They said there are others like them," the woman added. "They're calling them 'turning parties.' They just go around turning people back. Isn't it great? Maybe in a few years everything will be back to the way it was!"

Wayne continued past the couple without another word.

****

Wayne huffed and puffed, he wiped the sweat out of his eyes. Street after street passed him by, until he saw a small department store. He threw his backpack on the ground and ran to the window, cupped his hands to his eyes, and looked inside. It was full of zombies.

The door was automatic, but had stopped functioning who knew how long ago. He picked up a rock and hurled it at the door, smashing the glass. Inside, the zombies were grunting and turning toward the noise.

He jammed his machete into the nearest zombie, then rammed a knife into another one's brain. It hit the ground and he went down with it, stabbing through its skull over and over again, turning its head to pulp. He left the knife in the zombie's head and stood, drawing a 9mm from his side. Zombies approached from the aisles in neat little rows, almost like a shooting gallery. Wayne opened fire.

Every shot echoed across the store, rattling the shelves. More zombies came from the back of the store, drawn by the noise. Head after head rocked back with a bullet in it, zombie after zombie fell.

Wayne's gun clicked. He drew his shotgun and moved in closer, starting with the middle aisle. A zombie made a "Gletch!" sound as it lunged at him, but Wayne pulled the trigger and its head exploded. Chunks rained all over him. Wayne wiped his eyes, saw a rack of safety glasses beside him, and ripped one free and put it on. He went down the aisle killing zombies, stopping only to reload.

When the aisle was clear he switched to his revolver and started down the next. He hadn't practiced with it as much, so he missed a few times, but he had thinned down the crowd considerably, giving him ample time to reload. He emptied three loads of ammo from the revolver, then switched back to his knives as he rounded the corner and started down a third aisle. He stabbed a zombie in the face, it fell and took his knife with it, then Wayne grabbed a hammer from the shelf.

The next zombie to approach him got the hammer to the top of its head, and when it fell, Wayne hit it a few more times for good measure. He turned the hammer over and sank the pointy end into another zombie's head, and it reached up feebly as though it were swatting at a fly, then fell to its knees. Wayne took the zombies head in both hands, his thumbs over its eye sockets, and screamed as he squeezed as hard as he could. Something crunched and gave, his hands clapped almost together, and the zombie stopped moving. Wayne let it fall, then collapsed to the ground, his legs spread out before him, and screamed into the air.

When the echoes faded, the store was silent. Nothing moved through the aisles, the world may as well have been frozen. He sat there for hours.

As the sky was growing gray and his hands started shaking, cold from the blood all over them and the open door, he heard footsteps outside. The pattern was arrhythmic, coming from multiple sets of feet, and steady and fast. He heard glass crackle as they entered the store, then they came into view at the end of the aisle: a small group of people, probably bandits.

"Hold up," one of them said. The others stopped behind him. "You okay, partner? You bit?"

Wayne didn't look up from the mess of zombie head on the tile floor before him.

"You conscious?" a young woman asked.

"I think he's bit," one of them said.

"I ain't bit," Wayne said.

Their leader approached slowly, doing his best to avoid the bodies, and crouched down to meet Wayne's gaze. Wayne didn't let him.

"You do all this? By yourself?"

"Yessir."

The man looked the aisle up and down. "Not bad. It's no surprise you've lasted this long. Shame we didn't get here sooner though. There's a cure, you know. We could've helped these people—"

"Don't call them *people*!" Wayne screamed. He stared into the man's eyes, saw them widen, saw him raise his hands.

"All right, all right. Didn't mean any disrespect by it. You couldn't have known. Just… why don't we set you up with some supplies? We'll take care of you, sir, and you can retire—"

Wayne stood up and collected his knife from some zombie's eye socket. He grabbed a rag from one of the shelves and started cleaning it off. Most of the blood and chunky stuff had caked on there, but it came off with a little spit. "I don't need your supplies. I can fend for myself."

"Okay, okay. Again, we mean you no disrespect." The man turned to his companions, shrugged, and turned back to Wayne, who left the aisle to get the rest of his weapons from around the store. The group followed him.

"Look," the young woman said, "we're a turning party. We go around turning pe—zombies back into people. By biting them. That's how it works, you know."

"I get it."

"But biting them infects you, so you have to have someone bring you back."

"You ever think they don't want to come back?" Wayne said. He sheathed his machete so hard it nearly ripped through its holster. "You ever think they don't *need* to come back?"

"What's that supposed to mean?" a third man said.

"Everything happens for a reason. Even this." Wayne motioned around him.

"Some things happen for no reason," the leader said. "But sure, not this one. I think God wanted us to find the cure, and we did."

Wayne scoffed. "What you know about what God wants?"

The leader opened his hands to the sides. "I guess I don't know. I believe, though."

Wayne finished rounding up and cleaning off his weapons. He headed out the front door.

"Sure you don't want to come with us?" the young woman asked.

"Come with you? That's the last thing I want. Going around trying to reverse nature, trying to bring back these things, telling people how to live their lives. To hell with you all. I don't need you."

"I hate to keep bothering you," the leader said, "but what do you plan on doing?"

"None of your damn business."

The man looked to the side, at one of his companions. "I think it might be, actually. See, I have a feeling you're going to keep going around killing zombies. And I think that's wrong."

"I don't give a flying shit what you think."

"They can be people!" the woman said. "We can help them! You can't just kill them!"

"I can do whatever I want."

"You wouldn't go around a hospital shooting everyone with a cold, would you?"

"That's hardly the same thing."

"It's no different," the leader said. "These are people who are sick, who need our help. You can't just kill them."

Wayne drew his 9mm and turned. He aimed it at the leader's face, the young woman drew a knife, and another of the turning party drew a shotgun. The leader stood with his hands up.

"Easy now," he said to his friends. "Put those away." He turned back to Wayne. "Listen, partner—"

"Don't call me that." Wayne spat at the man's feet.

"What's your name?"

"Wayne Hewitt."

"Mr. Hewitt—can I call you Wayne?"

"I don't give a shit what you call me as long as you back off."

"Wayne, I think I get it. I know you don't want to hear that, but I do. For once in your life, you got what you want. The world left you alone, it left you to clean up and just do your thing. And you don't want that to change."

"Got what I *want*? You think you know me? Know what I've been through?"

"No. I don't know you, Wayne. But you don't know me, either. I'm not just some obstacle dropped into your life to trip you up. I'm going to reach into my back pocket, Wayne, will you let me do that?"

Wayne nodded. The man reached behind him, slowly, and took his wallet out of his back pocket. He held it out, his free hand still in the air.

"What you want me to do with that?" Wayne asked.

"Look inside. Please."

Wayne took the man's wallet and opened it. The center unfolded, revealing a set of photographs of the man before him, a young woman, and a little girl: A happy family, all smiles and swingsets and birthday cakes.

"That was my wife and daughter. Patricia and Bernadette. Named after Patty's grandmother. We called her Bernie. She was... seven when she died."

Wayne handed the man's wallet back to him.

"We tried to lock ourselves in our house when this all started, but you know how it goes. Staying put never works, they always find a way in. And they got Patty, and for a while it was me and Bernie. Until they got her too."

Wayne wiped his eyes and holstered his gun. He took his own wallet from his pocket, and the other gentleman raised his shotgun, but the young woman pushed its barrel back down. Wayne handed the leader his wallet.

"That's Shiloh. Her mother passed giving birth to her. I raised her alone, I taught her to play baseball, taught her to drive, how to shoot a gun. Not a one of those things helped her in the end."

"She was beautiful," the leader said. "I'm sorry for your loss."

Wayne's heart beat faster, he clenched his fists. "You know what it means to lose someone. So how do you go around *helping* these sons of bitches? After what they did to you?"

"Because they *didn't*, Wayne. One of them did, sure, a long time ago. But you can't hold the rest of them responsible. Hell, even the one that bit them couldn't help it. You were right, in a way. They aren't people. But they can be, Wayne."

Wayne turned away, his face red, his eyes watering.

"Wayne… they had families. Some of them still might. Don't you think we should give that back to them? Wouldn't you want someone to give Shiloh back if they could?"

"Don't you say her name!" Wayne shouted. He threw himself on the man, picked him up by his shirt. "Don't you dare say it!"

"I can't have Patty and Bernie back, Wayne. But this isn't about me, don't you see that? It's about what I can do for everyone else."

Wayne let the man go, he fell to his knees and cried. Between sobs he said, "I don't know what you want from me."

The leader put a hand on Wayne's shoulder. "We could use you, Wayne. Come on, come help us clean up. Help us give back. What do you say? Partners?" He held out his free hand. Wayne looked at it.

"Not now," he said. "I'm not ready yet. I'm not ready. I shouldn't even be here. It should've been me, not my Shiloh. It should've been me."

"But it wasn't, Wayne. You're still here. So please, make the most of it. Help us all make it worth it."

"It won't bring her back."

The man shook his head. "No. Nothing will, not now."

Wayne looked up at him. "You swear this works? You swear it changes people back? For good?"

"For good, as far as we've seen."

"I'll come with you," Wayne said. "I'm not ready to help yet."

"That's fine, Wayne. Just stay with us, help keep us safe, and watch. And whenever you're ready to do whatever it is you're going to do, we won't stop you. Deal?"

Wayne stood up. He dried his eyes, he shook the man's hand. "Deal. If it means I can help bring someone else's Shiloh back, deal. It's what she would want, I think."

"I have to hope so," the man said. "Or else I don't know what I'm doing this for. It's not for me, Wayne. It has to be for them."

"Yeah," Wayne replied. "For them." The leader turned and started down the road, and his companions joined him. Wayne took a last look at the store, then followed.

The After Life Part III: The Wilderlands

Audrey lay on her back, staring up at the photograph of Kenneth Warner. The fire was barely bright enough to illuminate it.

"If you stare at that picture long enough, maybe he'll come out of it," Jon said.

"Just thinking about what Dan went through to get this," Audrey replied. "How lost we'd be without it."

"Lost?" Xander said. He was stoking the fire. "Not lost. You saw that riot. We'll get our rights one way or another, and by the way that felt, not long from now."

"If they don't kill us all, you mean."

Xander shrugged. "We could always just leave."

"And go where? Where do people take their kids, their grandparents?"

"Avoiding the issue's no good," Jon said. "More normbies will just fall into the trap, it's a vicious cycle." The fire popped, and Jon put another stick on it.

"Wish we had had a chance to grab some popcorn on our way out," Brook said. "I'm starving."

"How much farther is the mall?" Jon asked.

"An hour, maybe two."

"Perfect. Nothing like dying on an empty stomach."

"Who said anything about dying?" Xander said.

"You think we're just going to waltz in there, grab the first zombie we see, it'll be Ken Warner, and we'll hop back out?"

"No, but it's not like we have no chance. Besides, we have each other. If someone gets bitten, we just change them back. No need to be so gloomy."

"I wonder how the others are doing," Brook said.

"They're probably at their mall already," Jon replied. "But they'll probably wait for daylight before they move in."

"I meant everyone back home. That was a nasty riot."

"I've been trying not to think about it," Audrey said.

"Oh, because of Dan?" Xander said. "Being commander of the guard and all—"

"Yes, Xander, that *is* what I've been trying not to think about. Thanks."

"Settle down, kids," Jon said. "Since we've got no food, why not pass the time with a story?"

"Storytime?" Brook said. She smirked, and hoped Jon could see it.

"Sure. I'll tell you about the time I got bitten. It was maybe three years ago—"

"That recent?" Xander said. "Seems like you've been with us at least that long."

"Time flies, I guess. I was with a small group of survivors, we were making our way south, trying to skirt the deserts. Guess we ran out of luck. We found the first small town we'd seen in days and headed right in. Walked right into a bandit trap. I remember gunfire, shouting, and we split up. I busted out a window of a house, what wasn't busted out already anyway, and I hopped in. I turned to look and see if they'd follow, and I backed right into a zombie. Bit down on me, right here." He tugged on his shirt collar and showed them the scar.

Xander was kneeling wide-eyed by the fire. "How'd you get away?"

"The thing had me held tight from behind, so I went back to the window and threw myself back on it. Leftover glass stabbed right into it, and I think I broke its back, too. Felt something pop. It let go, not dead but injured, and I pulled a bookshelf a little way off the wall and hid behind it. The bandits came by, killed the zombie, only gave a cursory glance inside the house, but I was hiding so long, I turned. I got out through that same window, with my old zombie friend to pad the glass, and off I went across the desert. I remember I was looking for other zombies to be with. It's like there's something that draws them to each other."

"If only humans had that," Audrey said.

"You don't feel drawn to Dan?"

"That's different, and you know it. When you're a zombie, it's almost like your body is just moving toward other zombies."

"Maybe it's the same and we just don't know how to recognize it."

Audrey laughed. "You're so romantic, no wonder Julia was willing to overlook your bite."

"She didn't overlook anything, she just doesn't care. From what she says, a lot of the humans don't. Only a few of them do, enough to keep trouble going for us. How about you?"

"What's that?"

"How'd you get bitten?"

"Oh." Audrey sat up. She leaned against a large rock circling their little campsite, tucked away between the rocks and hills. "I was skipping work that day. I wasn't sick, but my roommate was. I decided to sleep in, and I woke up to her breaking down my door. Before I could even get out of bed, she jumped at me." Audrey lifted her hands, her fingers spread wide to show wounds from a past life: Bite marks on her left hand, long, thin scars on her right. "Got my hand up just in time to keep her from biting my face. Smashed the lamp on my dresser against her head, but she wouldn't stop. I took a jagged piece of porcelain from the lamp and stabbed it into her neck."

"I'm sorry you went through that," Jon said.

"I turned before I figured out what was happening. A turning party picked me up and let me in on the loop. I eventually found my way to Breathaven. I remember I spent so long still feeling guilty for stabbing my roommate, no matter how many people told me it wasn't my fault. I still feel guilty sometimes. Never really had a chance to absorb what had happened."

After a while Xander said, "I was with a couple of guys from my school. Not my friends, but we happened to escape at the same time, and we just sort of stuck together. Had no desire to go our separate ways, that's for sure. But I was never one of them. They were friends, I was some guy they got stuck with. They gave me a portion of whatever we all found, but I was always the last to eat, the first to go into a dark room, and they were always making jokes about me. No better than high school bullies."

"Your bite's on your side, isn't it?" Brook asked. "I think you've shown me before."

"Yeah." Xander lifted his shirt, the scar was barely visible. If not for the tattoo, he'd be hard to pinpoint as a normbie. "We found this zombie one time, stuck in this pit someone had dug for it. They guys decided it was a good place to take a pit stop and tease me. Kept threatening to throw me in with it, then one of them lifted me by the shirt and held me by the ledge." Xander took off his glasses and wiped his eyes. "They laughed and laughed, and when I asked them to put me down, they just laughed more. Then my shirt tore. They dropped me right in, and the zombie got me. The guys just screamed and ran off. I never saw them again."

"How did you get out?" Audrey asked.

"My glasses broke in the fall. Not these ones, these are newer. I jammed the earpiece into the zombie's eye. Lucky for me I climbed out before I turned, or I'd probably still be down there."

"I'm surprised they let us have access to the eye doctor," Jon said. "Wouldn't put it past Warner to make up some bullshit reason why he can't get new glasses for normbies."

"I helped his guys set up the solar panels they use to light some of the buildings uptown. Otherwise, I'm not sure he would have."

"That leaves you, Brook," Audrey said. "You told us you got bitten in that mall. What happened?"

"I was just shopping."

"Oh come on," Jon said. "We all poured our hearts out. Your turn."

"Come on, it's only fair," Xander said. Jon led them in a quiet chanting of her name, and Brook rolled her eyes.

"All right. I was with my boyfriend. We were shopping in the mall, and somebody bit him. He was bleeding pretty badly, and people were shouting, pushing past each other… kinda like Town Square today, only surrounded by walls. We hid in a supply closet for a little while, and he passed out. I opened the door to see if it was safe to go get him help, next thing I knew he was grabbing me from behind, wrestling with me. At some point he bit me, right on my forearm. I guess that's when I realized he wasn't coming back, so I…"

"You didn't 'realize' anything, Brook," Jon said. "You just acted, you did what you had to, same as the other day. You didn't do anything wrong."

"I know, Jon. And thanks. But it still *feels* wrong. Anyway, I jammed my keys into his throat, over and over again, but he just didn't stop, so I went for his eyes. It's not like in the movies, he didn't just give up and drop dead. He kept coming even after I had… gouged both of his eyes out. He just wouldn't stop, he was still grabbing me, still biting at me, and then he just stopped, dead weight in my arms. Someone had heard us struggling and came in to help me, put a knife in his head. It was… hard for me to be thankful at the time, but it didn't matter. The guy took his knife back and then he was gone, and then I ran out into the mall. I wasn't even looking for anything, I was just running to run at that point, taking different turns, passing different stores. I got out somehow, I got as far as the parking lot, got inside my car, and then I changed."

"How long were you in the car?" Audrey asked.

"The whole time. My boyfriend, he was so picky about where he parked, he always had to park in the shade. He was right next to this building that caught the shade almost the entire day. If not for that, I would've cooked in there. It's like… I don't know. Like he saved me, even after he died. Even though I couldn't save him. I know that's stupid, it's just…"

"It helps give things meaning," Jon said.

"Yeah. Anyway, a turning party found me about a year ago, sent me straight for Breathaven."

"I remember the day you arrived. Took one look around and asked where to sign up for the uprising. I told you Earl's bunch was the closest we had."

Xander's stomach groaned, and the others paused, then laughed, all tension broken, all spirits lifted.

"I guess that's as good a place as any to try to get some sleep," Jon said, and he stretched out along the ground. One by one, the normbies fell asleep.

****

They woke up to thunder. Heavy rain came soon after, and though it was still dark, they started running.

Between the rain and the thunder, it was too loud for them to hear each other, so they just followed Brook. Soon they T-boned a street and ran down it, and the first building they saw was a little strip mall, its front windows shattered out. They stepped into the closest plot, formerly a video store, and moved to the back to keep out of the rain blowing in.

"How far is it?" Xander asked between breaths.

"It's not far now," Brook replied, "but we're going to need light. It'll be dark in the mall with no power."

"Think there's anything to eat around here?" Jon asked.

"There was an endcap for snacks up front," Audrey said, "but it was empty."

"Look." Xander was pointing to a door near the back of the store. "Employees only. Maybe someone left their lunch here."

"It'll be rotten," Jon said, "if not stolen. But it could be worth a look."

Inside the break room they found a few packets of hot cocoa, which, being scavengers through and through, they tucked into their back pockets. The fridge smelled so bad when they opened it,

Audrey nearly threw up. They closed it without getting more than a peek inside.

The next store over was a printing shop, and in the break room they found a box of cereal. It was half-empty when they got there, but they split what was left between the four of them. They didn't bother with the fridge.

The rain took a few hours to clear up, but when it did the sun didn't hesitate to reestablish itself. Jon peeked out through the window, then ducked back in. "We got zombies. Lots of them, a little farther down the road."

"Shit," Xander said. "What do we do?"

"We do our best to avoid them," Brook said. "This street is mostly strip malls and shops. It's laid out in rows, should be easy to stick behind buildings and make a straight line right for the intersection, take a right, and then it's straight on to the mall."

They rounded the strip mall they were in, doubling back the way they came instead of moving toward the zombies, and found the back alley far less populated. They moved quickly but soundlessly, pausing at the end of each building to look around the corner before crossing to the back of the next.

Ahead a zombie noticed them and started shambling their way. When it got close Jon sidestepped it, it lost its balance and stumbled, and Brook pushed it the rest of the way. They ran past without slowing: Jon checking the corner, the four of them running to the alley behind the next shop, rinse and repeat.

Jon sidestepped another zombie, ducking right into the space between shops, and a zombie grabbed him from behind and bit into his throat before he could raise his arms.

"Gack!" Jon shouted. Blood poured down his shirt. Audrey tackled the first zombie to keep it from joining in while Xander and Brook rushed to Jon's side. His zombie got a second bite in, then Brook punched it in the side of the head. The zombie didn't recoil. She shoved the wrestling mass of Jon and zombie as hard as she could, and they fell to their side. Jon rolled over the zombie, finally freeing himself of it. Xander grabbed Jon's arm and lifted it over his shoulder to help him walk, then cried out as the zombie bit into his leg.

Oh God, Brook thought, *I'm so sorry.* She stomped on the zombie's head as hard as she could, splattering it across the cement.

"Help me get him up," Xander said. He was limping, but still standing. Brook leaned down to help lift Jon, but then she saw his eyes, saw the way his limbs dangled, and tears started down her face.

"Xander, he's not alive."

Xander lowered Jon so he could look for himself, then covered his mouth. Audrey had backed the other zombie into a dumpster, and she shoved it over the ledge and inside with a metal *thund!* and then slammed the lid down.

"Fuck!" Xander shouted.

"Sh!" Audrey said. "They'll hear you!"

"Xander's bitten," Brook said. "We have to get him back."

"I'll get him back," Audrey said. "You keep going."

"No, fuck the mission, we have to—"

"Brook, you know where the mall is. One person will have a better chance sneaking around anyway. Just find Warner's son. All that matters is the mission."

Brook knew she was right, thought about going back empty-handed after losing Jon.

"What if I get bitten?"

"We would never leave you out here alone, Brook," Xander said. "Soon as we get back, we'll have Earl send someone out to meet you halfway, or find you and bring you back if you got bitten."

"Take care of yourself, Brook," Audrey said.

"Take care of each other," Brook replied, and then they split up. Brook continued along the alley as Xander's pained grunts faded away behind her. She had to keep clearing her eyes; she had held it together as long as she could, but now that it was just her and the zombies, she couldn't stop.

Brook reached the intersection and ran as fast as she could, the hardest she'd run since the day she was bitten. Zombies dove for her, but she stepped around them, charged through others. She zig-zagged across the street, down an alley between two fast food restaurants, and then entered another back alley. This one opened up much sooner, and Brook came out into the parking lot of the shopping mall.

Several cars still dotted the parking lot. Brook ducked behind one to catch her breath and give her legs a rest. She thought of Jon, held a silent memorial for him in her head, tried to hear what he'd say to her if he were beside her now. He'd tell her to keep going, tell her to find Warner's son and bring him back to change Warner's mind about normbies. He'd tell her he was right behind her. Brook started moving again as if he were.

She went from car to car to avoid being seen by the zombies in the parking lot. Some of the cars had shattered windows, all had flat tires from years of disuse. In the distance to her left was a familiar corner of the parking lot, and if she looked longer she'd see Bobby's car, where she had spent several years shuffling between the seats and pawing feebly at the glass. She turned her attention to the big double-doors ahead, one of the mall's main entrances.

A few zombies noticed her dashing across the lot and followed. Brook reached the main door, threw it open, and stepped inside. The door started closing slowly on its own, so Brook grabbed it and slammed it shut. A zombie smashed into the window on the door, threw itself against the door a second time, and then turned and shambled away.

She could hear moans and echoing footsteps as she ducked behind a planter with a small tree planted in it. The mall was dim, but a few feet ahead were the gory remains of a run-in with a zombie; most of the bones had been picked clean, the clothes shredded, but near the body of a dead zombie (*They won't eat their own*, Brook realized) was a blood-splattered aluminum baseball bat. Keeping low, Brook crept toward the mess and took the bat in hand, hoping she wouldn't have to use it. After what happened to Jon, she was more than prepared to, but she hoped it wouldn't come to that.

Brook froze for a second when she realized Audrey still had the photograph, but she shrugged it off. She had spent so many years staring at it, she didn't think it would matter. It was only a vague idea of what Kenneth Warner looked like, anyway.

The closest shop was a sporting goods store, which made her doubt the effectiveness of her baseball bat; that last person to wield it apparently didn't get very far. Brook moved across the walkway, still crouching, and stepped onto the padded carpet of the store.

Behind the counter, a zombie paced back and forth. He was wearing a uniform that matched the green of the sign above the shop's entrance. As quietly as she could, Brook stood and reached for the gate that would close the storefront off from the rest of the mall. She lowered it carefully, quietly, and while it rattled from time to time, it wasn't loud enough to gain any more attention than the odd groans and footsteps coming from outside.

The gate finally touched the floor, and Brook crouched again. She made her way through the aisles and covered herself with various knee and shoulder pads, leather gloves, and a hockey helmet and neck guard. As she strapped the helmet into place, the zombie behind the counter finally noticed her, and it grunted and groaned as it reached over the counter, not smart enough to simply fall forward over it.

The zombie was clearly not Kenneth Warner, so Brook headed for the gate again, now with almost every inch of her body covered. A zombie could still get a bite in, but the odds were less against her. She lifted the gate quietly, crept under it, then set it back down.

A zombie in a dress wandered the walkway ahead, just past the next store. Brook ducked behind a bench, waited until it was looking the other way, and rounded the corner into the store. It was a glasses shop, but it was empty. Brook looked across the aisle at the opposing store: A small soft drink bar with no access into the shop except through a door to the side. As far as she could tell, it was empty.

The zombie woman noticed Brook as she was leaving the glasses store. The zombie grunted and started for her, tripped because of her high heels, and fell on her face. From above and behind her, Brook put the bat between the zombie's jaws and lifted her to her feet, then wrestled her over to the soft drink bar, where she tossed the zombie over the counter with a thud. The zombie reached and reached, but Brook crept away.

Next to the soft drink station was a coffeeshop. Brook peeked around the corner and saw three zombies. One was a young man wearing jeans. He was facing away from her, but worth checking out. Brook sneaked back to the sports shop, grabbed a baseball, and went back to the wall between the coffeeshop and the drink bar. She took the baseball and threw it as hard as she could at the gate of the sports shop. The ball struck the metal gate and sent a ripple through it, rattling loudly and echoing through the store. One of the zombies let out a "Yeh!" of surprise, and all three started toward the sports shop. The one in jeans was the last out, and as he passed through the opening, Brook stepped forward and brought the bat between his jaws. He grunted and groaned, but no more than he already had been, and Brook pressed him against the ground, a hand on either side of the bat.

Though his face was sunken from years of malnourishment, the man looked twice her age. His nose was far wider than young Kenneth Warner's, and his eyes were blue, while Kenneth's were green. Not him. Brook grabbed the zombie and raised him to his feet, then shoved him toward the drink bar, where the nicely dressed lady zombie was still reaching over the counter. The man bumped against it, and Brook grabbed him by the pants and lifted him onto the bar, then toppled him over it. After that she sneaked into the coffeeshop while the other two zombies smacked and pressed against the gate of the sporting goods store.

Brook walked quietly between sets of tables and chairs. She felt something on her leg and looked down. A zombie she hadn't seen lying under a chair bit down on her leg, but its teeth stopped on the shin guard she'd put on. Brook yanked her leg free, her knee guard slammed into the nearest table, and it fell over with a crash. Several distant zombies grunted their notice. Time to run.

Brook headed out of the store and ran down the aisle, sizing up every passing zombie as quickly as she could: Too tall, this one a woman, that one an old man, wrong hair color, not wearing jeans. There were so many of them. Brook headed for an escalator; who knew how long ago it had stopped working, but she hoped the stair-like passage would give the zombies trouble all the same.

The escalator slowed the zombies far more than it slowed her, but on the second step from the top, Brook's toes caught on the edge of the stair, and she tumbled onto the ground of the upper floor. She tried her best to roll to avoid twisting anything, and when the world stopped spinning around her, she realized she was looking at a supply closet, its door held slightly open by a leg, not eaten from at all. She recognized the shoe immediately, and froze. Then she heard Jon's voice in her head: *Leave it in the past, Brook. You have to keep going.*

Zombies moaned and snarled from behind and below her. Brook stood up to run, and almost tripped again. Her shin guard had twisted around her leg, all but preventing her from bending her knee. She tried to straighten it but separated the buckle instead, and the shin guard came off. Brook kicked free of it and headed for a store ahead of her, a clothing shop that looked empt y. Two zombies approached from the side, cutting off her escape. She turned from them and started down the next lane instead. A zombie appeared before her, and Brook shoved it over the alley's railing, where it fell to the floor below.

The next shop was a small diner full of zombies. At cursory glance, none of them looked like Warner. One came forward, and Brook smashed the bat into its head, not hard enough to kill it, but hard enough to send it sprawling. The next threw itself at her, grabbing her arms before she could set up again, and they tumbled over the railing. Brook grabbed onto the thick metal bar, and her arms hurt as she caught herself from falling. The zombie clawed at her but only skimmed her pants as it fell.

Brook pulled herself up, got one arm over the railing, and then a zombie sunk its teeth into the gap between her glove and her elbow guard. Brook cried out, punched the zombie with her free hand, and then she fell.

Pain shot through her head as her helmet cracked against the ground. Brook moaned, looking around. There was blood everywhere, but it was coming from the bite in her forearm. She heard grunting; the zombie that had fallen earlier was crawling toward her, both its legs fractured. Her ears were ringing, her head was spinning. She tried to sit up, but for a second couldn't tell whether she was face-up or face-down. Brook relaxed, let her head rest against her helmet resting against the ground.

Get moving, she thought to herself. *They'll come for you, but you have to be alive. They don't eat their own.*

Brook shoved herself forward and sat up. The crawling zombie was a few feet away, and Brook shuffled backward until the disorientation left her, then forced herself to her feet, turned, and limped away. Her arm was throbbing, her head was throbbing, and her leg was sore, but she hadn't broken anything. Most of the zombies were still struggling on the escalator behind her, some of them shoving each other off of it.

A zombie came in from the left but tripped over a planter. Brook shuffled to her right to stay out of its reach as she passed it, lost her balance when pain shot through her leg, and tumbled. She pushed herself toward the nearest store's opening so she would land mostly out of sight and hopefully on carpet.

She was rolling again, and this time she landed on her stomach. Brook raised her head enough to see two pairs of legs walking toward her. A zombie woman in business attire was a few feet ahead, behind her Brook saw a pair of jeans, a young man with green eyes and brown hair. She pushed off of the ground and onto her feet, grabbed the businesswoman by the forehead and neck, and shoved her away. Then she dove forward, grabbed Kenneth Warner's arm, and bit into it.

Brook had been lucky and got him from behind. She shoved him forward, and he crashed to the ground. Brook returned to the businesswoman zombie, who was getting back up. Brook grabbed her by the hair and pulled back to keep her from clenching her teeth, then guided the woman toward the front of the store. She shoved her outside, then yanked down on the metal grating of the gate, which crashed to the ground and echoed through the shop.

She took a look around. She was in a hair salon, and at the back was a payment counter. Bleeding and bruised, Brook limped toward it. Kenneth Warner's zombie lunged at her as she went, and she sidestepped him, barely avoiding his gnashing teeth. Brook reached the counter and threw herself over it, hoping she hadn't just taught the zombie in the room to do the same. Lying on her back on the ground behind the counter, Brook tore the hockey helmet off of her and breathed deeply, staring at the dim ceiling.

Brook could feel herself fading, a feeling that was suddenly familiar to her, like falling asleep with her eyes open. Then she heard groaning, movement, and then a voice.

"What happened?"

Almost too tired to care, Brook sat up. "Are you Kenneth Warner?"

"Yeah, I'm Ken. What—" He retched a few times, then threw up on the ground.

"I need you to bite me."

"What?"

"Not now, after I change. Do you remember being bitten?"

Ken held his head, he looked around. Several zombies had gathered at the gate and were pounding against it. "I remember those."

"If you get bitten, you turn into one. But biting them turns them back, only it re-infects you. I bit you, and when I turn into one of them, I need you to bite me."

"I'm not staying here," Ken said. "That gate isn't even locked—"

"They won't figure out how to lift it," Brook said, though she was starting to worry about that herself. "Please, I need you to—"

"Shut up," Ken said. "I don't know you, I'm sorry, but I'm leaving the first chance I get."

"I can get you out of here, just like I got in."

Ken pointed at her arm. "Looks like that worked out great for you."

"Yeah, well, you didn't exactly escape unbitten the first time you tried either, asshole."

Ken's eyes widened. "Where's my dad?"

"I know him, I know where he is—"

"Bullshit."

"Hugh Warner. I can take you there, but you have to wait for me to turn and then bite me."

"Jesus, you're like a broken record," Ken said. He leaned against the counter, right in front of her. "Where's my dad?"

Brook realized she was rocking back and forth, trying to force air in and out of her. "Promise me."

"Where is he!"

"Bite me," Brook said. She took one last look at the world, then fell backward and stopped moving.

"Hey," Ken said. "Hey, wake up!" He looked at the gate; more of the creatures had arrived. The bottom of the gate rested an inch above the ground, and he thought he saw it climb a little higher. "Hey, wake up, don't leave me alone in here!"

Ken wandered the salon looking for something he could use to defend himself, but found only old bottles of hair product, brushes, and combs. He tried spraying hair spray in a zombie's eyes, but it didn't even flinch. Ken sat in one of the styling chairs, then he heard a moan coming from beyond the counter. He turned to see the girl from before lifting herself up, but now she was just like them, groaning and reaching for him, not smart enough to get past the counter.

He thought about what she had said, thought about what he'd been doing the past… how long? He remembered it all: walking the halls of the mall, people coming in at some point to look for supplies, those same people not getting very far, climbing up and down the escalators. He remembered the day the lights went out and the escalators stopped moving, he remembered even further back, back to when the clerk first attacked him, to getting separated from his dad, Ken remembered finding a coat hanger and untwisting it and jamming it in the clerk's eye.

Everything she had said seemed to be true, but that meant bringing her back would change him. He didn't want to be one of *them* again, couldn't stand the thought. Ken got as close to the gate as he dared, looked for some means of escape. No supplies, no idea which way the exit was, no idea what to do if he got to it.

"God damn it," Ken said. He went to the back of the store, where the girl reached for him, her dead eyes never moving from him. Ken grabbed her hand, pulled a little to keep her arm taut. She swung the other around wildly, without control. Ken took a few deep breaths, closed his eyes, bit down on leather glove. He spat the taste out of his mouth, let go of her hand, and paced a little line near the back of the store. He wished his dad were here, then he wondered about his mother. Where was she in all this? He hoped she was okay.

She needs me, Ken thought. *Why else would she come all the way out here alone? If I turn back, she'll turn me again. My dad must've sent her to help. Everything will be okay. Besides, she got bitten for me.*

Ken went back to the girl behind the counter, raised her hand again, pulled her glove free, and bit down on her skin, lightly at first. Then he looked at the blood all over her forearm, thought about how hard he'd been bitten by the clerk, and bit harder, hard enough to draw blood. She showed no sign of feeling any pain, anything at all really, and then Ken let her go.

Between a group of zombies at the gate and one behind the counter, one he had put all of his faith in, Ken sat down on the floor of the salon, and waited.

A Really Long Walk

Do you remember the first time we met? I asked you. You were shaking, feverish, lying there in your sleeping bag near the fire. You somehow found the strength to nod your head.

Yes.

It was that little park across from the café. I used to get coffee there, sit in one of the patio seats, hoping to meet someone.

You never met anyone there.

No, I didn't. Eventually I started crossing the street and jogging through the park. It was a shortcut home at first, but then I started jogging the whole track because it helped me clear my head.

I was always… that bench.

Yeah. You were always sitting in the same bench, even that first time I took the shortcut home. Never said a word, just watched me jog by.

You didn't reply. You had stopped shaking, too.

One day I stopped jogging, and I asked you what you were doing. And you said 'clearing my head.' I thought that was funny. We were both there for the same thing, but we did it in a different way.

You groaned.

I think that's sort of how we've done things ever since. After the same thing, but we have a different way of going about it.

You sat up, you turned to me.

It kept things interesting. Most people, that would push them apart, drive a wedge between them. For us it was glue.

You leaned forward, moaning, your teeth clamped down on nothing. The face mask pressed against my skin, and you couldn't get within an inch.

Do you… ever get tired of doing this? I asked you. Your teeth clicked together, pulled apart. You raised your hands, but they were tied together, useless to you. I took your hands in mine, those hands I always loved to hold, even in that moment, and I bit down on your shoulder. After a few minutes of gnashing and pawing at me, you fell back down, you fell asleep.

Because I do, I said.

****

Good morning, you said. I could tell you were afraid, so I smiled.

Good morning.

I was worried you'd turned already.

I'm surprised I haven't. I feel fine, actually.

You took the mask off of my face and untied my hands. We made breakfast together.

I'm glad, you said as we ate. Seems like lately we turn so fast, we hardly get more than a few minutes together.

I didn't say anything for a while. When I finished my beets I said, It's hard.

What's that?

Never seeing each other for more than a few minutes. Maybe an hour. You should've woken me up, we'd have had longer.

You looked so peaceful. Like you were tired. I didn't want to wake you.

Thanks, I guess. I could always sleep while you're… you know, though.

You gave me a look that said I'd crossed a line, but then you smiled it off. I like watching you sleep, you said. I miss that.

Oh. I'm sorry.

Don't be sorry. We don't have time to waste being sorry.

Isn't that the damn truth.

We spent almost two hours together before I turned. That was the longest we've had in a long time.

I woke up with your arms around me. You didn't have the mask on. I sat up so fast it woke you. You rolled onto your back, rubbing your eyes and yawning, then said, It's early.

You don't have the mask on, I said, and you winced. You tried to play it off like there was just too much light for your eyes, but I could tell. I mean, it's just… we have to be careful. What if you turned before I woke up, and bit me? What if I didn't get a chance to bite you back? We'd both…

You sat up and stared toward the window, the tiny ray of light squeezing in through the boards over it. We'd both turn. I sat down beside you. You turned and looked me in the eyes. Would that be so bad? you asked.

What are you saying?

We'd be together forever. No more worries.

That's bullshit. We might not stay together at all, we might head in different directions.

They stay together. We've seen enough of them to know that. They're better at sticking together than the normal ones.

I don't want to be one of them, I said. I refuse to believe you do.

I don't, you said. I just think about things, when I'm alone. While you're out. I guess the world will do that to you. How long has it been since we've seen someone else?

Too long. I started stoking the fire, then put a pot on the grate over it.

We should get moving, you said. It's been long enough since we've moved, maybe this whole thing is over. Maybe someone's found a cure.

Maybe there's nothing left out there, I replied. Maybe civilization is done for and we're the last two people on earth.

You wrapped your arms around me from behind, and my heart jumped. You pressed your cheek into my back.

That wouldn't be so bad, you said.

No, I replied. If we didn't keep turning, it would be wonderful.

You didn't reply, so I stopped making breakfast, laid you down on the bed, and put the mask on your face.

****

The next time I woke up I heard screaming. My head was ringing, and I sat up. It wasn't you screaming, it was the tea pot. What day was it? Had to stop the sound, it might draw unwanted attention. Why would you leave it on? You must've turned quickly. You must've felt it coming at the last minute, because you had the mask on. You weren't tied up; you were wandering around our little shack. I'm lucky you didn't notice me sleeping there; you could do enough damage without your teeth.

I snuck up behind you and grabbed you by the wrists. You pulled and wriggled but I held you tight, bit into your back.

I could feel myself turning before you passed out, before I could take the mask for myself. Had to think fast. I gagged myself with an old shirt as tightly as I could. I think I fell asleep crying thinking about how I didn't get to see you at all that turn.

****

I woke up all alone. It was worse than waking up to screaming. I called your name, I searched what little space we had in the shack, then I went outside.

Winter was creeping up on us. I sat outside among the trees, watching my breath in the early morning air. I heard a little rattling, and you came up the hill carrying firewood. You were wearing the mask, and a new kind of fear came to me.

What if you had turned out there?

You walked right past me, into the shack. You worry too much.

If you had turned I never would've found you.

I didn't go far. If I started to feel myself turn, I would've come straight back here.

Next time you go for firewood, just leave me out. Bite me when you come back. I don't want to lose you.

You won't lose me. Jesus, we haven't lost each other yet. When did you stop trusting me?

Don't make this about trust. Please. I'm afraid.

You hugged me. You held me close, you kissed me, and you said, Don't be afraid.

But I'm always afraid.

****

I decided to leave you out. It hurt so much, closing the door to you wriggling around like a maggot, moaning and clattering your teeth together.

I went down the hill, toward the road we first spotted the shack from. I walked for miles along it, but then a fog set in and I couldn't see anything. The world was so goddamn quiet out there. No shuffling feet, no distant cars, definitely no roar of planes above the clouds. Just miles and miles of utter nothing.

I came back up the road, to the little tree where we carved our initials in case we ever couldn't see the shack. I opened the door to check on you and regretted it immediately, because the sight hurt just as much the second time. I closed the door and headed past the shack, toward the little house it belonged to.

The door was broken, like it was when we found it. I tiptoed around the broken glass and into the dark back room. I went from hall to hall, room to abandoned room, not sure what I was looking for.

Upstairs I found a picture that had been knocked from the wall. A trail of blood dried years ago streaked down the wall, starting near the nail the picture once hung from and ending toward the floor. There was a spot here and there along the wall where the injured person had used it to prop themself up. Any other remnants of that ancient struggle were gone, except maybe the smashed-in glass door, but that might've been looters long after.

The glass of the picture was cracked. The picture inside was warped from being exposed to the air for so long. It made me think of how you and I never had a chance to buy a house together, to hang pictures of us along the walls. Honestly, I couldn't even remember if there *were* any pictures of us, just you and me.

I went back out to the shack and I bit you, and when you stopped thrashing around I covered you in a blanket, put the mask over my face, and shivered myself to sleep.

****

I went for a walk the other day, I said. You laughed.

That doesn't sound like something you'd do.

No. I guess I had to. I don't think we'll last the winter.

We can move into the house. Cover up the broken door.

We'll probably have to. Anyway, I did like it. The walk. It was nice.

Find anything out there?

Nothing. No town, no cars, no people, no zombies. I think we're alone on this mountain.

I think we're alone in the world.

We sat side by side, near the fire. You started shaking, not just because of the cold, and I sighed.

Sorry, you said. Guess I'm turning early.

Don't be sorry, remember? You can't control when you turn.

No, you said. But you control when I turn back.

What are you saying?

I wouldn't blame you if you ever thought about taking a walk. A really long one… the kind where you don't come back. I'll admit I've thought about it.

Of course I've thought about it, I said. Something like that would've scared most people, but not us. I felt the warmth that only comes with that kind of blatant and open honesty. God, we were good.

You would never do that to me.

I don't think you'd do it to me, either.

I go on walks all the time, you said. Once a month, maybe. I make sure you're settled in and I walk around out there.

I thought about it, recalled vague memories of you leaving. All the days blur into one now, even the ones where I'm not out.

You ever see anything?

You squinted your eyes, looking up at the ceiling. My second walk I saw a zombie. I decided to turn and run back home.

This isn't our home.

You're my home. I came back and bit you and went to sleep praying it wouldn't find us. Of course it wouldn't; it was miles away. Even if it had heard me sneak off it would've gotten lost trying to keep up. But at the time I was so scared.

You shivered again. I held you close. You kissed me, then reached for the mask and put it on, leaned your head on my shoulder.

That's all this is, you said. Life. Just one long walk to the grave.

I don't like it when you talk like this.

Do you remember that shitty movie we watched one of the first times we went out? Where the girl dies at the end, and the guy decides she lives forever in his heart?

Yeah.

I always wanted us to live forever, you said. Then you went out.

****

I could walk so far. I could walk so far and never come back, never bring you out of this. Not just walk to find a town or a person or a cure, but walk to find myself free of this back-and-forth responsibility, our daily hour-if-we're-lucky life together. I could leave for years and come back and find you still writhing there. Not mad at me, not upset with me, just writhing there until I decide to bring you back. I could leave for years and never come back at all.

But then I'd be free of you, and that's no way to live.

I took off your mask and let you bite me.

We have to do this right, so I couldn't risk you eating me before I regained consciousness, or whatever semblance of it zombies have. I knew it might not work, but I had to leave the little shack.

I put tape on the door so it couldn't click shut; the door would just push open. I cut off some of the skin on my side and tossed it into the corner of the shack to distract you, then I went out through the door. I could already feel myself fading.

I found a bell in a box of Christmas decorations in the basement of the house, and I tied it to the outside of the shack door, so it would ring if you came through. Then I moved tables and couches around inside the house so that I couldn't get anywhere but that back room, with the broken door. I took old tin cans and hung them up from the broken back door, so they would clatter together if I came out. Now if either one of us decided to leave, the other would hear. We would find each other.

I fell asleep in the back room, smiling despite the cold, the shaking I couldn't stop. We would find each other again, and you and I would live forever.

Diminishing Returns

"He's turned," Polly said.

Linn had already felt it, and tightened her grip on Tim's arms. "I got him."

Tim sat up, groaning. He saw the other three ahead and lurched forward, but didn't get far; his legs were stretched ahead of him, Linn kept his arms behind him, and he stretched and leaned forward but was nowhere near close enough to bite anyone.

"Guess I'm up," Andrew said. He kneeled in the road and raised Tim's pant leg. Years of scars adorned Tim's calf and thigh. Andrew bit into Tim's leg until blood trickled onto the asphalt, then he let go, sat up, and wiped off his mouth. "Damn, it's like biting into a leather jacket. Maybe we should consider retiring."

They all had the same scar pattern, some on a leg, others an arm. It was part of the cost for what they did: Linn, Tim, Polly, Andrew, and Duane were a turning party.

"Whatever," Linn said. "Just get the mask on him and let's go. There's a lot of daylight left."

Duane and Polly strapped the mask over Tim's mouth, then Linn let go of his arms. Phil lunged at Andrew as though he wanted revenge, but the metal wires of the mask kept his teeth two inches from Andrew's shoulder.

"Bet you can't wait for him to wake up," Duane said to Linn.

"It's not like we hate each other." Linn stood up and dusted off the back of her jeans. "Anyway, I wouldn't wish this on anyone."

"Maybe you could be a two-person turning party," Andrew said. "Then you'd never have to deal with each other for long." He tugged on the rope affixed to the mask's collar, which made Tim start walking toward them.

"That would be complicated. And it leaves way too much room for mistakes. Jeez, we look like dogs when we're under."

"It does the trick." Andrew pulled on the rope again. "He really wants to go that way."

"Must be zombies out there," Polly said. "Probably close, if he'd rather go be with them than try to eat us. We should be on guard."

They moved off of the road and into the field, where the grass had been uncut for years and now brushed against their waists. They let Tim guide them, moving in the direction he tugged, every now and then stopping to wait for him to get tired of trying to bite them and resume pulling in the direction of other zombies. It was a slow process, but like a lot of slow processes, it was one that worked.

The group reached the outskirts of a town at nightfall. Quietly, they broke into the farthest house they saw. Polly watched from the window to make sure no zombies were coming, and Andrew, Duane, and Linn broke out their map.

"Where's the nearest settlement?" Duane asked.

Andrew pointed, and Linn saw his finger was shaking. "Here. The houses on the little island, remember? It's not too far. We should probably pass through, actually, in case they have anyone who needs turning."

"We can bring someone with us, then," Linn said. "There's bound to be zombies in town. We should turn one or two of them."

"Tomorrow?" Duane asked.

"Tonight." She nodded at Andrew. "His hands are shaking."

"Caught red-handed," Andrew said. "Or shaky-handed. Yeah, I feel it coming on. Might not be a bad idea to bring a person or two in here and turn all of us at once, then take them to the island with us tomorrow afternoon-ish."

"Tim will be up any minute," Polly said. "Someone stays here with Andrew, the rest of us head out as soon as he does."

"Good plan," Duane said.

"Ask Tim first," Linn suggested. "He might be tired, might want to stay."

The group took a rest in the dim house, and Linn found her way to the next room, where she sat on her knees and said a silent prayer. Soon she heard talking in the other room.

"Welcome back," Polly said.

"We staying here tonight?" Tim asked.

"That's the plan," Andrew said. "We're actually doing a run to turn some zombies. You can stay here and watch over me when I turn, if you want."

"No thanks. Feels like I just woke up, I'm ready to go. Where's Linn? She doing her thing?"

"Quiet," Polly said.

"I'm right here," Linn called. She stood up and joined the others in the living room. "Who's staying with Andrew?"

"Doesn't matter to me."

Linn looked at Duane. "Guess I'll stay," he said, "unless you want to."

"You can stay," Linn said. "Let's gear up. Grab a couple extra masks."

"Take mine." Duane handed Linn the zombie mask out of his backpack. "Don't bring back more than three people. I don't think we could handle it."

"I don't either. You two ready?"

"Born ready," Tim said, and Polly nodded. Linn opened the front door, and the three of them stepped into the night.

****

Linn, Tim, and Polly sat on the roof of a one-story building, looking over the edge at the town below. The only light came from the moon; more stars than the three of them had seen in their lives now shone nightly, unimpeded by pollution or city lights.

Habitually, Linn reached up and put her hand around the cross hanging from her neck.

"Talking to your imaginary friend?" Tim asked. Polly nudged him hard with her elbow.

"Those three," Linn said. "Sort of cut off from the rest. Right by the streetlight in the road."

The others looked. "There are closer ones," Tim said.

"Not if we take that alley right there." She pointed. "We come up from there, mask them from behind, drag them back in, and then we just walk them around to that street over there." She turned to their left and pointed. "Leads right to the house we're staying in."

"I like it," Polly said. "Should be a breeze."

"Not bad," Tim said. He stood and headed for the ladder on the back of the building. "See if you guys can keep up."

They crept up the back alley, hoping the trio was still there. When they reached the end they saw the fallen streetlight, and the three zombies still standing by it, one of them swaying slightly in the warm breeze.

"Masks out," Polly whispered. Each of them took a mask, and Tim went out first. He headed for the nearest zombie, came up behind it, and slipped the mask over its face. It snarled, but the mask muffled most of it. The other two zombies turned, but Linn side-stepped to stay behind hers and drew a mask over its face.

Tim was already halfway to the alley. Linn dragged her zombie backward, and that's when she saw Polly struggling with hers. Linn checked the alley, motioned to Tim that she had to go help, but then Polly's zombie slipped free. With a loud "Reeeahhhhhhh!" It started shambling toward Linn. Two more zombies emerged to see what the fuss was about, and started shambling toward the turning party.

Polly came up behind her zombie and slid the mask onto its face, but now most of the zombies on the street were heading right for them.

"Damn it!" Tim said. He looked to the side. "That door!"

Polly reached the door first, threw her zombie down and put a foot on its chest, then tried the knob. "Locked!"

"You're bleeding," Linn said.

"He bit me, worry about it later!"

"Next one!" Tim said. Linn marched her zombie toward the door of the next building, even though it meant heading toward the oncoming zombies. One reached it almost as soon as she did, and Linn shoved her zombie forward, using it as a shield. The other zombie reached around at her, but lacked the motor skills to find anything worthwhile. Linn tried the knob and the door opened. She shoved both zombies hard but held tight to hers, and the other went sprawling. Linn threw her zombie into the room, then held the door open wide. Polly and her zombie shambled inside, followed by Tim and his. Linn slammed the door shut at his heels.

Polly already had a flashlight out. She was checking the corners; they were in some kind of diner.

"Is it empty?" Linn asked.

"Shh!" Polly replied. She pointed forward; the front window of the shop had been smashed in. Besides the gaping hole in security, the place was empty.

"How bad is the bite?"

"Not bad. He nipped my arm a little. We'll just have to turn me too, it's not a big deal."

"It is if we can't get back," Tim said. "We need a plan. That street's not empty."

"There are zombies further into town," Linn said, "but we can outrun them."

"With three zombies? I don't think so. Besides, we don't know if the other streets are even clear. Those zombies back there had to come from somewhere."

"Maybe we should cut our losses," Polly said. "Leave these three here and head back to regroup."

Linn and Tim looked at each other. "I don't like it," he said. "This is our job. If we go back now, there's no guarantee it'll be any easier later. Plus it throws us off schedule."

"Okay, then what do we do?"

"Press on," Linn said. "We head out right through that window and check the street. If it's not clear, we head for that library right across the street. Looks like two stories. Even if it's not empty, we should be able to make it to the second floor and barricade the stairs. That'll give us time to watch the street for an opening and get back to camp."

"What if Polly turns?"

"What if she doesn't, Tim?"

"Then we'd be lucky."

"Do we have any more masks?" Polly asked. "Never mind, I can just gag myself if I start to slip."

"Let's do it then," Tim said. "The longer we wait, the longer we're exposed." He crept toward the front of the store, but came back when he was only halfway. "Too many of them, they'll see if we try to peek at the road."

Linn went to the wall and crept along it so she could get farther without being seen by the zombies on the street. She made it to the front of the store, then came back. "I saw movement. Can't say much more than that."

"If it's just one or two, we go down the street. Any more, we head for the library."

"Deal," Polly said, and they picked up their zombies and headed for the gaping hole in the window.

There were five zombies on the street, and one of them noticed the group almost immediately. The party headed across the street instead, right for the library's front door. Beyond it was a tiny lobby that consisted only of the door they came in through, two walls, and another door leading into the main floor. Tim tried the knob, but it was locked. It had a little window in it, so Tim reached into his pack. He put on a leather glove padded with gauze with a small metal plate in the front, then smashed the window in, took the glove off, and reached in and unlocked the door. They entered the library, and Polly pushed her zombie away and then grabbed a nearby cart, which she wheeled in front of the door to slow any zombies that might follow them.

"Check the aisles," Linn said, and one by one the group of three people and three zombies wriggled through the library looking for zombies. Each passing second brought relief, as any zombies should've heard the glass break and come running, but it also brought panic; Polly could turn without notice, and they still had to wait for the street to clear.

"Good news is we can watch from the ground floor," Tim said. "I'd hate to see an opening from up there only to lose it by the time we got down here."

"Bad news?" Linn asked.

"Bad news is I don't feel so hot," Polly said. She choked a little, like she was stifling a cough. "Worse comes to worse, you guys leave me and these three here and go get Duane."

"You'll be fine," Linn said. "We got this far into town, we can get back out."

"Yeah," Polly said. She sat down against a bookshelf, then jerked her zombie to the ground. It fell, sat up, then pressed its face against her shoulder, completely harmless thanks to the mask.

Tim whispered to Linn. "I don't think she's going to make it."

"She's my best friend. I'm not leaving her."

"We would come back, Linn. Use your head. We could be back here with Duane in an hour."

"Then how much longer until she turns back?"

"Who cares? Andrew will be fine on his own, and Duane will turn all four of them. If we're lucky, all of us sneak out of town mask-free and get back to camp by morning."

"If we're lucky," Linn said. "If we're not, they'll turn at different times, and we still have to wait for an opening, and all of that time will have been wasted."

"Look, you don't want to leave her, I get that. I'll go myself." Tim started toward the door.

"Wait," Linn said. "You're right. Kind of. But you don't have to go all the way back and get Duane just because it's his turn. I'll bite them."

Tim grimaced. "You just turned back yesterday."

"Whatever. Has to happen sooner or later. It's all luck of the draw anyway."

"What's up, guys?" Polly asked. She was sweating, straining to keep her head up. Linn and Tim worked their flailing zombies into the aisle and toward her so they could talk.

"I'm going to bite these three," Linn said. "Then you, once you turn. That way, with a little luck, the five of you can sneak back to camp by tomorrow, and you only have to worry about me."

"That's a good plan," Polly said. She flashed Linn a thumbs-up, then her hand and her head dropped.

"Better get to it," Tim said. "And… thanks. For volunteering."

Linn raised her shoulders. "You just got back a few hours ago. It's only fair." She bit into her zombie, then Tim's. Polly's zombie sat up, no longer trying to bite at her through the mask.

"Finish that one," Tim said. "I'll tie Polly up real quick." He took a scarf from his bag and tied it tightly around Polly's mouth. If she tried hard enough, she might still be able to bite through it. Polly's head raised, her eyes opened, and she groaned. Tim pushed against both of her shoulders to hold her down, while the other three zombies moved in, grabbing at his arms and neck and pressing their masks against him. "Try to find something we can use to tie them down!"

Linn shoved between the zombies and ran to the small room behind the reception desk. There were all kinds of office supplies inside, and in a filing cabinet she found a bundle of zip ties. Linn brought them back to Tim, and the two of them took a nearby book cart and rolled it to the end of the aisle. They managed to sit Polly down by it, and they tied her hands around one of the cart's leg poles. The next zombie was easy, and once they had him tied on the opposite side of the cart, neither he nor Polly could move it without pulling at the other. The other two zombies were easier to tie to it, but by the time they finished, Linn could feel herself starting to shake.

The four zombies couldn't maneuver the cart very far, and they definitely couldn't figure out how to work it into an aisle, so that's where Tim and Linn sat down, breathing heavily.

"Hope one of them turns before you do," Tim said. "I need another mask."

"We have more scarves."

"Yeah, but that means I can't sleep. I'm damn tired."

"Oh, sorry." Linn looked at the zombies. Only two of them were facing toward her, Polly and another woman, and their eyes longed with hunger. "I hope they turn back soon, too."

"How do you still believe?" Tim asked. Linn turned to him, and she realized she was holding her necklace again. She let her hand drop away from it. "After all this? Your friend sitting over there, like… *that*. All the times it's happened to you. What God would do this to us?"

Linn didn't want to respond. Her hands felt hot, all the classic arguments rushed through her head, but she ignored them. "We're still alive, right?"

"Tch," Tim said. "I guess."

He let it drop after that, and Linn was glad. She looked at the zombies from time to time, and finally she sat up. "Hey, one of them stopped moving."

"Good," Tim said. "You okay over here? I need to get over there and make sure nobody flips out as soon as they come back. I'll get a mask on you as soon as I can."

"I'm good," Linn said. Tim nodded, then left her alone in the aisle.

****

Linn came to in the old house. Everyone was packing up to leave, and she was lying on a couch. She sat up.

"Hey," Polly said. "We made it back okay."

"Everyone?"

"Yeah. The other three turned fast. Duane bit you."

"He didn't have to do that."

"It's all right," Duane said. "I wasn't looking forward to another march just yet anyway, figured I might go under and spare myself. Guess I wasn't so lucky."

"Well, we're all awake now," Tim said. "And these three are starving. Let's get to the island."

They finished packing up and headed out. Somewhere in a field a hundred feet from the abandoned highway, Tim walked with the map spread out in front of him. Finally, he stopped.

"What's the deal?" Duane asked. "We should keep going, I'm starting to feel it."

"We will," Tim said. He pointed to a small spot on the map. "We ever go through this town?"

"Don't think so," Polly said.

"Maybe we should check it out after we drop these three off. Look where it is, it's close to all our other stops but it's sort of all on its own out here."

"It's out of the way," Linn said. "So maybe there's something worthwhile there."

"We can check it out," Duane said. "On our way back."

"Sorry to slow you down," one of the newcomers said.

As Tim folded the map and put it away and they all started walking again, Linn said, "I didn't catch your names."

"Brianna."

"I'm Evan. This is Johnny."

"You knew each other?"

"Not really," Johnny said. "We went to the same school, saw each other around town sometimes. Gotta say it's nice to see a familiar face out here, though."

"Yeah," Evan said.

"Any of you have families?" Andrew asked. "Back in town?"

"My brother," Brianna said. "He was with me when this all went down. No idea if he's still there."

"Throw together a description or a sketch. We'll look for him next time we pass through. We always give priority to family and friends of people we already brought back."

"And when we get to the island, don't eat too fast," Tim said. "You'll rupture your stomach."

Duane fell to his knees and threw up. The others stopped and waited for him; Linn put a hand on his shoulder. When he was ready he took her hand, and she helped him up. Tim offered him a mask, and he put it on.

"So you guys just wander around turning people back?" Evan asked.

"Yeah," Andrew said.

"That's badass. Listen, back in that town, I had nothing. No family, didn't really know anybody but my coworkers. I was a mechanic, mostly worked on cars and bikes. Can't imagine that's too useful out here. Why don't you let me come with you?"

"Thanks for the offer," Polly said. "We'll keep it in mind. For now you're going to need to stay on the island until you're in better health."

Duane turned after sunset. The moon offered enough light to see when it was out, but clouds pressed in and reduced their sight to fleeting windows. They found a little dip in the field, and waited around to see if Duane would try to head out in another direction, but he only lunged at the members of the turning party and the survivors, so the group deemed it safe enough to set up camp.

"Whose turn is it to bite?" Tim asked.

"Yours," Polly replied.

Tim frowned. "Already?"

"We got thrown off schedule," Linn said. "Messed us all up."

"Well, if it's my turn, it's my turn," Tim said. He reached for Duane, who they had hog tied and put on his side, with their bags around him to keep him from writhing too far.

"Wait," Andrew said. "Might as well get some sleep tonight and wait for morning. With luck we'll all be sober and we can reach the island by noon."

Tim shrugged. "Works for me."

"We don't have to take a turn, do we?" Brianna asked.

Linn shook her head. "Wouldn't do any good to have non-members change back. Our job is to turn people and get them to safety."

"Is there any food?" Evan asked.

"A little," Andrew said. He went for his backpack, careful not to let Duane free.

While the others ate a light ration and conversed, Linn watched Duane, his vacant eyes lit by the fire, so glazed they were almost white. She tried to remember her time as a zombie, not just the latest but all of them: Wandering around, reaching at anyone normal, tugging toward a direction for what seemed like no reason, only when she was awake she knew it was because that's where more zombies were.

Linn was thankful she hadn't been killed before the cure was discovered. So many zombies had fallen in the years after the first bite, and those ones couldn't come back. And who had figured out they could come back, anyway? Who woke up one morning and decided to bite a zombie? It was all so convenient, it made no sense. Linn held firm to the concept of evolution, but there had always been things that, to her, made no evolutionary sense. Morality was one of them; altruism was the very antithesis of evolutionary survival mechanisms. Evolution said procreate and exist at all costs; altruism told soldiers to throw themselves on top of grenades to save their brothers-in-arms.

This was another thing that didn't make sense. One day, certain people changed, and the dead walked the earth for years, but all along they held the secret that a bite would change them back. If evolution was a room full of monkeys eventually churning out Shakespeare, biting zombies was someone coming in and changing the ending. There had to be an outside influence, or it didn't make sense.

Or maybe the whole thing made no sense all along. It worked for her, it helped her sleep at night, it unwound all of the knots in her personal theory of everything, the one that just couldn't stand the thought that everything happens for no reason and every person on this shaking earth is, was, and will always be alone, until they simply are no more.

Linn looked at Tim, already sleeping a few feet away. She didn't hate him, but she couldn't understand why he felt a need to constantly dangle scissors around those threads, and dreaded the day one of his jabs finally made the whole thing collapse.

****

In the morning Tim bit Duane, and the group slowly progressed toward the island. Duane turned back a few hours later, which sped their pace slightly, and in the afternoon they came upon a place where the ground sloped downward toward a river.

"There's the island," Andrew said. He pointed to a little bar of land in the middle of the river, closer to one side than the other. It was close enough to the other side that a person could swim there in a matter of seconds, but the zombies had never figured out how to cross it.

On the little strip of land were seven large houses, probably someone's vacation home way back when. There had been a bridge to and from the island, but its inhabitants had long since torn it away. The remains were charred, the remnants of some great battle now a passing sight one might miss if they didn't know where to look, or care about things that happened a long time ago to someone who wasn't them.

For now, there was—

"The boat," Polly said, pointing. It was hidden among the rocks and covered with a camouflage net. As small as the boat was, it held the eight of them well enough, though Tim's shaking made the trip bumpier than any of them would have liked.

They touched land on the island, where a dirty, scar-faced man had already come out to meet them.

"How's it going, Hubert?" Duane asked.

"Can't complain. These three new recruits, or just new?"

"Just new," Polly said. Hubert didn't move.

The group got out of the boat and Andrew and Tim pulled it onto land. Evan's stomach groaned loudly. Linn said, "How are you doing, Tim?"

"I have another hour in me, at least."

"How much food do you have?" Andrew asked Hubert.

"Enough to take on these three. Scavenging's been dry lately, but we catch enough fish, and there's game in some woods a few hours away. And the gardens. We'll manage."

"Might not be for long," Duane said. "Evan here wants to join us. We'll probably pick him up next time we're through."

"That reminds me," Linn said. "Can I see the map?" Tim handed it to her. She unfolded it and approached Hubert, who looked as though all human beings exuded five-foot pins and needles only he could see or feel. She stopped a foot away and pointed to the mystery town on the map. "What do you know about this place?"

Hubert reached out and took the paper, looked it over, then folded it and handed it back. "Small town. Not a lot of people there. We haven't scavenged over that way, not that I know of."

"We're adding it to our route," Linn said. "It might be a little longer before we're back here."

"Sure," Hubert said. "We'll miss you. Oh, here." He dropped a burlap sack at her feet. "Not much, but it's a little food we could spare." Hubert turned to the three newcomers, who had already figured out to keep their distance. "You three. This isn't free. You stay here, you work. We have crops to tend, we have watches to make sure nothing gets in. This island is safe, it's secure, but only because we make it that way. You want to stay, you gotta help. Yeah?"

"Yes, sir," Johnny said, while Brianna nodded and said, "Uh-huh."

"Thanks for the food," Andrew said.

"Thanks for the recruits," Hubert replied. "You need medical supplies?"

"Not this time."

"You have any extra?"

"Can't say we do. You need something specific?"

Hubert shook his head. "Just checking. Anything else?"

"Think we can stay for the day? Tim's gonna turn soon."

"Maybe we should keep going, actually," Polly said. "Plenty of light left."

"Won't reach your next stop before there isn't," Hubert said. "Doesn't matter to me. Stay or go, just let the watchman know." He looked at the three survivors, then jerked his head backward. "I'll give you the tour." The four of them walked up the little beach toward one of the mansions.

"What's our next stop?" Andrew asked.

Linn looked over the map. "If we want to check out that town, we should do it next. We'd only be going farther, so it's either now or we check it when we swing back around."

Tim coughed a few times, wretched and spat on the ground, then said, "Any objections?"

"I'm fine with it," Duane said. Andrew nodded.

"All right. We'll check out this town and see what we see."

The turning party got back into their boat and shoved off of the island.

****

Dear God, Linn thought. She paused for a long time, unsure of what she wanted to say. *Help us help them*, she finished, then let go of her necklace.

Their feet dragged them across miles, sometimes finding a rest stop by the cracked and useless highway, sometimes sleeping below the stars. They had one small tent in case it rained while they were out, and it was only meant for two people, but all five would squeeze in, even whoever was taking their turn as a zombie.

One night Linn sat near the fire, her pant leg lifted to see the web of scars on it. The latest bite was just starting to scab over.

"How long do you think it'll be?"

"Hm?" Polly asked. Linn looked up, realizing she had spoken out loud.

"Will we find a real cure? So we don't have to spend a fifth of our lives dead?"

"We're not dead. Just asleep. Who knows."

It was a small price to pay, really. One little bite every few days, in exchange for giving the gift of life back to others. That didn't make it easy.

"We should reach town by tomorrow," Polly went on. "If there are zombies there, we should have no trouble keeping…"

"It's your turn next."

"…*me* going toward it."

They turned in for the night. In the morning Polly turned Andrew back, and the group went on toward the town. They reached it before Polly started shaking, and stopped a few hundreds yards away from it. Tim had the binoculars, and he stared across the open field at the outskirts.

"Whole town is maybe a mile wide," he said. "Full of zombies. Right there though, see that flat grey building, with the orange dots?"

"I see it," Duane said.

"That's a personal storage complex. We should head straight there, it has a nice fence around it. I guarantee the place is empty and secure. We can make that our base camp."

"Good idea," Polly said. "Let's get there quickly. Hand me a mask."

Duane gave her a mask, and she put it on, then coughed a muffled cough. The group crossed the field toward town, crept along alleys and beside overturned cars, and eventually came to the fence of the storage. They went around toward the gate, which was closed and locked with a padlock and chain. Their bolt cutters took care of the chain, and when they were all inside, they put the chain back around and locked it with a lock of their own, one they held the combination to.

Andrew tapped on Linn's shoulder as she spun the dial on the padlock. She looked where he was pointing and saw a few zombies pressing against the fence, hitting it from time to time.

"So they know we're here. They'll forget when we break eyesight, though." She glanced up at the razor ribbon adorning the top of the fence. "At least we didn't have to try to climb it."

They rounded the first corner and entered an aisle of storage units. One by one they checked the rows, but the place was barren.

"This place is secure," Tim said. "Very. The units go right up against the fence in most places; it's not coming down anytime soon, and if it does, it'll be small enough to bottleneck them."

"Maybe…" Polly took a deep breath, panting through her mask. "We should look for…" Her shoulders slumped, her head drooped. Andrew tightened his grip on her rope.

"Keys," Linn said. "She was going to say we should look for the keys."

"Not a bad idea," Tim replied.

Right by the gate was a little booth barely big enough for them all to stand in. It was divided into a small space for the person operating the gate, and a back office for paperwork, a water cooler, and the keys. These were kept in a drawer, each key in a little packet with the number of the storage unit written on it in big bold marker. Tim emptied them into his bag, and the group filed out of the office.

Outside, Polly was leaning against the gate, occasionally smacking it, trying to get out to join her zombie brethren. Linn stared at her for a second. Why did the zombies do that? The only thing stronger than their urge to eat human flesh was their urge to be with other zombies. What force drove that? Evolution maybe; strength in numbers. But as far as she knew, no other creature did anything like this. How did we go from humans to… this?

For all their flaws, zombies stuck together better than people ever did. No reports of zombies dividing off into factions or waging war, no reports of zombies eating each other.

"Linn?"

"Yeah?"

"Can you get her? We should tie her down before she draws more with the noise."

They hog tied Polly, put her in one of the aisles, and then set to exploring the storage units. There wasn't much of use in them; mostly furniture, books, old clothes, video tapes, broken things.

"Not much in the way of scavenging," Duane said.

"But as a base camp it's perfect," Tim replied. "It's secure, out of the way—"

"We can save everyone," Linn said. The others turned to her. "We can clear out the town. Bring everyone here, put them in the storage units. Then we just gather food, clothes, everything, and then wake them up."

The others looked at each other, or away. "It's risky," Andrew said.

"Look at the payoff, though. A whole town turned back in one go. And another settlement on our map we can bring people to. Do you know how long it would take to keep coming here, grabbing three or four zombies at a time, turning them, and bringing them to another town? Telling them to wait in some place that isn't their home while we eventually find their loved ones, months or years later? But in a few weeks, a month tops, we could have this place up and running, and nobody wakes up miles from home with people they've never met."

Duane cleared his throat, but didn't say anything. Andrew looked away. Polly grunted.

"I think she's right," Tim said. All eyes were on him. "It's more efficient. It just makes sense."

"I see the logic," Duane said. "But what about the other settlements? A whole month behind schedule?"

"We can do it," Andrew said. "We don't all have to be here. We split into groups."

"There are five of us. If we split up, that means we have a pair. We don't do pairs."

"No," Linn said. "We don't. So whoever splits into two heads back to the island and picks up Evan. So we have three people here while the other three run our normal route. It'll help us build a stockpile of food and supplies around here anyway."

Duane rubbed the back of his neck. "Okay. Yeah, it makes sense."

"But?" Andrew said.

"It's risky. Three is small. Accidents can happen."

"Accidents can happen with six," Tim said. "They *do*."

"We don't have to decide right now," Linn said. "It's getting late, we can sleep on it. Besides, we could never make a group decision with somebody under. We need Polly's input."

"Yeah," Andrew said. "Just give it fair thought. Everybody."

Everyone nodded their agreement, then they set up camp between two rows of storage units and eventually fell asleep.

****

In the morning Tim bit Polly, since he was still firmly in the "let's do it" camp. It didn't matter; she came to before he went under. After talking it through, they decided to go ahead with the plan.

They spent a day gathering zombies from the town and locking them in the storage units. It took some practice, but between the five of them they learned quickly.

The next morning Duane and Polly decided to head back to the island to get Evan. The group gathered at the gate to say their goodbyes.

"Sure you don't want to stay?" Linn asked.

Polly shook her head. "You know me. I can't stand staying still. Will you be all right with Tim?"

"I can handle Tim. Besides, we have a lot of work to do. We'll be all right."

The two met in a hug, then let each other go. Tim unlocked the gate, and Duane and Polly disappeared into the distant landscape. Meanwhile Linn, Andrew, and Tim got back to work.

On the road they would wait until morning to bite each other, but that often wasted the day out here, so they did it before bed in hopes the other person would wake in time to work in the morning. One night Linn came to long before dawn. She opened the door of the unit she called her bedroom as quietly as she could; it still screeched on its hinges as it went up, but she needed the fresh air.

Linn stood in the aisle of the storage staring up at the endless stars. A tiny drop of liquid hit the pavement and soaked into it.

"Can't sleep?" Linn turned around fast, then settled down when she realized it was just Tim. He was sitting by a little campfire, probably keeping watch even though it didn't seem necessary.

"Yeah. Just came back."

Tim nodded. "You should get some rest. We still have a lot of work to do."

Linn sat by the fire. "The work we do. It's good work."

"Yeah. It is."

"Why do you do it? Why'd you become a turner?"

Tim took a deep breath, looking up, lost in memory. "I didn't have much else to do. Figured I could be helping people."

"Me too. And I guess it feels like I should."

"Should? Oh, I think I know."

"Yeah."

Tim stoked the fire. "If there's a God, would he want you to drive yourself into the ground? Or rest? God rested on the seventh day, or so I've heard."

"I think He'd want me to keep going. As hard as it was."

"Maybe he would. Maybe he'd want both, Linn. For you to keep going, but to rest when you decided it was enough."

"Maybe."

A zombie pounded on the door to one of the units. A few others took up the protest, but after a few minutes without other stimulation, they gave up and went back to silence. Linn spoke again, quieter.

"I feel like every time I die, less of me comes back."

"Then stay here, Linn. Once we finish this. Nobody would blame you."

"There are still people out there to help. So many of them."

Tim nodded. He stared into the flames, then he chuckled. "Maybe that's why bad things happen in the face of God. Maybe he has to take a break too." He stood up. "Put that fire out if you go to sleep. And you should, Linn." Tim went back inside his storage unit and closed the door most of the way. It didn't make a sound.

****

Two weeks later Duane, Polly, and Evan came by with a wagon full of food. They stayed overnight, and in the morning headed out again. Linn, Tim, and Andrew kept at their own work, until the days grew shorter and yielded fewer zombies to store in the units. The moans and rapping against the storage unit doors grew too loud, so all three decided to stay in a nearby house. They needed the last three units for the rest of the zombies anyway.

They had gathered everyone, as far as they could tell, when two days went by without a single zombie; they walked the streets of a tiny ghost town where garbage blew in the wind and mailboxes drowning in grass leaned after years of neglect.

Late in the afternoon Duane and Evan returned with more food. Linn didn't need to ask where Polly was; she could see it in their faces. *Accidents can happen.* Alone in her room that night, she said a prayer, clutching her necklace so tightly she accidentally tore it from her neck. In the morning she tied the remains of the chain to fashion a bracelet and got back to work.

It took another two weeks to turn everyone back. The hard part was guarding the food to make sure it lasted and that nobody ate too quickly.

One day it simply occurred to them that their work was done. Everyone was turned back, only two people had died trying to get back to health, and the town was running almost the way it had before.

Andrew was under, and it was Linn's turn next. Once she had taken care of him, she went into a room alone to pray. Tim was waiting when she came back out.

"We're heading out tomorrow," he said.

"Yeah," Linn replied.

They sat together in a dark room. There was no power, they spoke by candlelight.

"You're not coming with us, are you?"

"I don't think so."

"I'll tell the others. It's good, Linn. You've earned it."

"I don't feel like I have."

"You saved a whole town."

"I couldn't save Polly."

"It wasn't your job to. It wasn't your job to save the town, either. You just did it. Sometimes things happen, Linn. There doesn't have to be more to it than that."

"I guess not. But it scares me."

"It scares me, too."

"How do you get through it?" Linn asked.

"Polly died. Whether there's a God or he has any power or he cares at all, it still happened. So did saving the town. The world spins on, Linn. I just have to believe everything will be okay, and if it isn't, then I'll react to it the best way I can. And if it helps you to feel like something has your back, if that gets you through it, I think that's okay. I guess there doesn't need to be more to it than that."

"For now, at least," Linn said.

In the morning they gathered in the road they'd come in by. One by one, Linn said goodbye to her friends. When she got to Tim, she hugged him.

"Be safe out there," she said.

"Be safe in here," Tim replied.

"If you ever get tired, you know where to find me."

"I do."

One by one the turning party headed down the road, back into the wilderness, back to work. Linn started in the other direction, back into town, to get some rest.

The After Life Part IV: Back From the Dead

"I know there's no good way to say this," Audrey said, "but we have to go faster."

"We'll make it," Xander said. He was shaking, Audrey could feel it. He was leaning against her, one arm around her shoulder, to keep the pressure off his leg. "We just might have to move in the dark for a while."

The sun was setting, and Audrey was trying hard to remember the way back. The tall grass was parted somewhat, so she stuck to that, but if they had passed their campsite from the night before, she hadn't noticed.

Audrey's eyes darted back and forth, and she realized she wasn't looking for Breathaven, but for something she could use to muzzle Xander. She shivered thinking about it; for now he was still her friend, and he might even make it back to town. The sun was almost gone, and then the field parted and they came to a river.

"D—downstream," Xander said. "We must've gone a little wide coming back."

"Almost home, Xander," Audrey said. "Hang in there."

They limped along the river until it joined up with the one surrounding Breathaven. When they reached the short hop across, Audrey set Xander down, made sure he couldn't roll into the water, then crossed alone. She came back with a sturdy enough sheet of metal, helped him limp across to the bus, then picked up the metal, sidled around Xander, and set it back down on the other side so they could finish crossing.

They came into the slum and found it empty. The gate into Town Square was open, and Douglas was standing on top of it, rifle in hand.

"Audrey! Where the hell—"

"He's been bitten," Audrey said.

Douglas looked around to make sure no one was watching, then came down off the gate. "I'll get him to a confinement cell and make sure he's taken care of. You get to Town Square."

"Is there a meeting?"

"Public execution."

Audrey handed Xander to Douglas, who carried him toward a door just beyond the gate into uptown. Audrey approached Town Square, where a large group of people and normbies had gathered. All of the guards except for Douglas were posted around the crowd to keep another riot from happening. In place of the podium was a large gallows, where a man was standing with a noose around his neck. Hugh Warner was standing next to him, shouting.

"…stand accused of attempting to murder me. How do you plead?"

"Does it matter? You're gonna hang me either way."

"I'm not pleased with killing anyone," Warner said. "Mankind needs all the number it can get."

"Remove restrictions on human-normbie relations, then."

"Those restrictions are for the safety of everyone. You're derailing the trial."

"Trial? You already have the noose around my neck!"

The crowd roared its agreement, though a few booed.

Warner shook his head. When the crowd was quiet, he said, "Peter Moynahan, I hereby sentence you to die by hanging for inciting a riot and attempted murder. May God have mercy on your soul."

The crowd erupted, some shouting "Kill him!" while others pushed against the guards in useless attempts to rescue the normbie. Warner crossed the podium to a large wooden handle, took it in both hands, and for a moment the whole world seemed like it was in free-fall. Then, Warner let go.

"I can't," he said. "We are too few already. I can't kill him."

Any booing from the crowd was drowned out by applause.

"You sure?" Peter said. "I won't think twice about trying to bash you over the head with that bottle."

"Revenge led humanity down a dark path, once. Let us forge a new path in peace. Peter Moynahan, I sentence you to a year of returning duties. It will be your job to bite any citizens or wilderlanders coming in bitten. You'll spend a great deal of this time as a zombie, and after your sentence you'll be returned to your home—"

"Back to my slum with all the normbies I've created for you to step all over!" Peter shouted, but Warner only spoke louder over him.

"To your home a free man, though I'll make sure the guards keep a tight watch on you for the remainder of your days. Take him to confinement."

The crowd shouted and jeered and some applauded, while two guards led Peter toward one door and five guards led Warner to another. After that, the rest of the guards ushered the normbies back toward their slum.

Audrey found Earl in the crowd. "Earl."

"Audrey? What's happened?"

"Jon's been killed in action. Xander got bitten, I brought him back, we just came in. Douglas took him to confinement until he can be turned back. Brook is still out there."

"You left Brook out on her own?"

"We were right outside the mall, Earl. We didn't want Jon to die for nothing."

Earl shook his head. "Now we might lose both of them for nothing. You don't get to make those kinds of calls, you hear me?"

"If Brook wanted to come back with us, she'd have come back with us. You want to make the calls, why don't you go out there?"

They walked in silence until they reached headquarters. Earl stopped outside the door and stared Audrey down.

"That wasn't fair of me," she said. "I'm sorry."

"It's all right. We're all on the same team, here. Unfortunately, I already have Bryce and Sebastian out scouting for food, and Whitney and Kirk are in confinement. We're stretched thin as it is."

"You're not going to send anyone out for Brook?"

"None of the recruits are ready yet, especially for that mall. We're going to have to wait until someone comes back."

"She could die!"

"I know that, Audrey. I just don't have anyone I can send out now. If I did, they'd be out already."

Earl went inside HQ. Audrey walked the streets of the slum, saw kids playing with rocks in an alley, a man cooking most of a rat on a spit. She waited by the alleyway that led into the slum, hoping for some sign of Brook. The muscles in her legs screaming at her were the only things keeping her from heading back out. That, and she didn't know the way.

Long after the sun had fallen, she heard the sound of metal bending in and being walked on, and then four people appeared in the dim light: Nora, Lyle, Stacy, and Cody. Audrey searched hopefully for a fifth person, but no one else crossed the little metal bridge.

"We searched the mall through and through," Lyle said. "Wasn't very big, but we spent all day looking. Must've searched every zombie six times, none were him. How'd you get back so fast?"

"Xander got bitten," Audrey said. "I had to bring him back."

"It's okay," Nora said. "Brook and Jon are our best scouts, they'll find him."

Audrey grimaced, and the four of them exchanged glances. "Jon… didn't make it. He got bitten, badly. Lost too much blood."

Tears appeared in Stacy's eyes. Cody clenched his fists. "What about Brook?" Lyle asked.

"She pressed on. We were right outside the mall when it happened. We need to go back out and meet her halfway. Either she found Kenneth and they're on their way here, or she's been turned and she's stuck there. Either way, we have to help."

Cody sat down as though the thought of walking all that way already wore him out.

"We need to eat," Lyle said. "We haven't had a bite in days. Then we can head straight out." He looked at the others. "Right?"

"We have to wait for morning," Nora said.

Audrey turned on her. "Every minute we stay here—"

"You're going to cross the wilderlands? At night? You know the way by heart, Audrey? Because you won't be able to see the map. We're just as likely to pass Brook by coming home. We wait for daylight, we get some rest, and we follow the path you took *exactly* to make sure we aren't dancing around each other out there."

Audrey leaned against the wall, then slid down it. She put her face against her knees and cried.

"I know it's hard," Lyle said, "but she's right. We have to wait."

"Just a few years ago, I could've called her on my cell phone," Audrey said. "We could've driven there in twenty minutes."

"That's not the world anymore, Audrey."

"I know." Audrey stood up and helped Cody rise as well. "Everyone eat and get some rest. We're leaving to find her at first light."

"Maybe we'll get lucky and she'll come in during the night," Stacy said.

"Yeah," Audrey replied, but she had stopped believing in luck a long time ago.

Normbies!

Caretaker

Hard dog food clattered as it entered the empty bowl, then the noise softened as it piled up. Hoyt Reiner shook it to level the food out, put the bowl on the ground, and then whistled. "Here, boy!" he called.

Hoyt set the bag of dog food on the counter, then looked around the dim house. "It's awful lonely up here," he said. "Better get back to work."

He went out through the front door into the crisp mountain air. The view was ecstatic, but without anyone to share it with or comment on it, Hoyt barely noticed anymore.

It was from that same viewpoint Hoyt watched the world end. He could see the city at the base of the mountain, and from above it he watched the fires, explosions, and a plane crash; from the wooded mountain he heard gunshots, screams, the occasional boom, and then, worst of all, silence. Years of it.

For a long time he was afraid to light a fire, worried that the smoke or even the light could be seen from town, might draw those things in. Eventually winter came, and he had little choice: Light a fire or freeze to death. So Hoyt lit a fire, and nothing came up from the town. The mountain must've been too treacherous for them, or maybe there weren't any left. Either way, he made sure to only light fires at night if he could, and always covered the windows with thick curtains and blankets if he kept a light on inside.

Life for Hoyt returned almost to normal. Every morning he woke up, fed and watered the dog, then went outside to tend the crops. Not a lot grew in these mountains, but Hoyt had moved up here to write, gotten bored and taken up gardening, and eventually found himself good at it. With the world ended now, his writing was worth nothing (except for the occasional maintenance of his sanity) but the growing was worth everything, and it became his primary hobby. Besides, with no electricity, what else was he supposed to do?

The cold nights were the worst. The fireplace kept the chill at bay, but there was something about those nights that made Hoyt's son act up. He would rattle his chains, throw himself against the walls of the shed, moaning and groaning all night. Those things people became didn't seem to feel pain, but it sure sounded like Justin was suffering out there.

Justin was only eight when he was bitten by his mother. Hoyt had watched the whole thing in horror, and while he tried to call the police only to find a dead phone line, Helen had attacked him, too. He tried to talk her out of it, and he knew now he never had a chance. Once you turn, you turn. In the end they had wrestled around the living room, Justin crying and bleeding, and they bumped into a table and knocked a vase over. Hoyt had taken a shard of the vase and jammed it through Helen's face, and just like that, she died. No lingering, no death throes, just gone like a light going out, leaving Hoyt with a scar on his hand and his son passing out from blood loss. Then Justin got up, moaning and writhing like Helen had, but Justin was smaller, easier to manage. Hoyt had chained him up the shed until help could arrive. It never did.

Year after year, Hoyt's hope for a cure grew along with the peppers and lettuces and beans in the back yard. He grew plenty of food, more than enough to last him all year, and the woods provided enough game, as long as he didn't hunt too often or in the same places. Animals, thank the Lord, weren't affected by the blight. They could be killed by the infected, but they never turned, so their populations stayed high enough. Hoyt tried to hunt different animals each year, but, as in all things, sometimes he had no choice.

The days blurred into each other like breath from his mouth in winter, or even in early spring or late fall. Wake up, feed the dog, tend the crops, pace the house, pretend Justin's quiet.

One morning Hoyt woke up like he had every other day, but something had to change. He stared at his watch, watched it pass two, three, then four minutes past the time he normally got up.

Then Hoyt lifted himself out of bed, went into the kitchen, picked up the dog bowl and emptied it into the trash, then set it on the counter. He filled the bowl with food, set it down and whistled, then went outside to tend his crops. Soon it would be too cold for them to live, but he had already harvested most of them, and the rest would be ready soon. Hoyt went back inside, scooted a chair across the main room, stood on top of it, tied his belt onto the ceiling fan, looped it at the end, and slipped it around his neck.

Hoyt leaned forward, enough to pull the belt tight, enough to put pressure around his throat. His toes kept him still on the chair, still breathing, and he waited. The ceiling creaked a little, then settled, and the distant rattle of chains from the shed broke through the otherwise silent house.

"I'm sorry, Justin." A tear fell to the ground, parted the dust Hoyt no longer bothered sweeping up. "There's no one coming for either of us. I'm sorry I couldn't help you."

Hoyt stepped forward, the chair tipped over and out of range of his feet, and the ceiling fan tore free from the ceiling with a crash, wooden ceiling fan blades raining down around him, bits and particles of ceiling scattering across the floor and into his hair and mouth. Hoyt spat and shook his head, snorted the dust from his nose, and sat up. He looked at the mess he'd made, the wiry tangle in the ceiling, and stood and dusted himself off. Hoyt untied the belt from his neck and went to get the broom.

****

From then on, Hoyt decided if he was going to live, he was going to enjoy it. He lit fires even if it was still daylight or the windows weren't covered, he ate when he was hungry, he visited Justin every day. Hoyt would sit cross-legged and talk to his son, and though Justin never did more than pull his chains taut and groan, Hoyt enjoyed their time together. Maybe one day he would hear Justin speak back to him again.

One foggy morning in the middle of spring, Hoyt woke to Justin having one of his fits, only it was louder, clearer than normal. Hoyt tore himself from the bed and ran to the window. He could see the shed's doors were open. He grabbed his shotgun and ran out back, up the small path toward the shed, his heart racing.

Hoyt rounded the shed doors and lifted his gun. A young man and woman were facing away from the doors, toward Justin, but they turned when they heard him approach. Both raised their hands, and the woman tucked a young child behind her legs.

"Wait!" the man said. "We didn't mean to intrude, we were just scavenging!"

"What are you doing in here?" Hoyt shouted. "That's my son!"

"We weren't going to hurt him, I swear," the woman said. "We saw smoke a few nights back and came toward it, hoping to find shelter, maybe a safe haven."

Hoyt lowered his gun. He could tell they were terrified, especially the young kid, who barely peeked out from behind mother's jeans, with wide eyes, and hair cut short. Hoyt sighed. "Come out of there, you don't want to get close to Justin. He's... not quite right. We can talk inside, where it's warm."

Hoyt led them along the path. He opened the back door, then crouched down to meet the child's eyes. "What's your name, kid?"

"Samantha."

"Samantha, go on in, okay? I promise it's safe in there."

Samantha ran in through the back door, and Hoyt stepped in front of it before her parents could follow. "Hold up," he said. "Just need to check you for weapons."

"My wife has a crowbar," the man said. "I have a revolver in my holster."

Hoyt looked the two up and down, pinpointed the weapons they'd mentioned. "I see them. You're not going to use them, are you?"

"Not if we don't have to."

"All right." Hoyt stepped aside and let them into his home.

"You're very trusting of us," the man said.

"Worst you can do is kill me," Hoyt replied. "But I imagine you don't want to."

"Thank you," the woman said. "For letting us in out of the cold."

"Yeah, it gets nasty up here, even in summer sometimes. Living room's this way. I'll put on a pot of coffee."

Samantha and her mother sat in the living room, but the man followed Hoyt into the kitchen. "Thanks again for not shooting us," he said. "We were just passing through, looking for somewhere safe."

Hoyt started a fire in a little trash can and put the small metal grate he used as a stove over it. A light draft spread out near the wall where a series of piping carried most of the smoke outside, but the fire quickly drowned it out. "Well, there's no safe haven, if that's what you wanted. My house is safe, isolated. You're the first people or… not-people to come up here." He filled a pot with water and set it on the stove. The man's wife entered the kitchen, and Hoyt emptied the dog bowl into the trash and set it on the counter. He filled it with food.

"What are you doing?" the man asked.

"Feeding my dog."

"But—"

The man's wife took his hand, and when he met her eyes she shook her head slightly. Hoyt set the dog bowl down and whistled, then turned to the couple. "Not much coffee left, might need to make a run into town one of these days. I've tried weaning myself off the stuff, but it's one of life's last pleasures, isn't it?"

"If you're going into town, I can help you," the man said. "I'll come with you, watch your back."

"Never really needed help before," Hoyt said. "Guess that don't mean I never will, though. I imagine you want something in exchange, yeah? Saw my garden on the way along the trail, right?"

The man grimaced and put a hand on the back of his head. "Yeah… It's hard for me to ask this, but could we stay here for a couple days? Even just the night? We've been traveling so long."

"You climbed a mountain," Hoyt said. "If you weren't already tired, you must be now. So yeah, you can stay. Come with me into town tomorrow and get some supplies, and you and your family can stay the week."

"You have yourself a deal, mister," the man said. He held out his hand. Hoyt shook it.

"Name's Hoyt."

"Bill Moore."

"Addy Moore, and you've already met Samantha."

Hoyt nodded. "The boy out there is Justin. My son. You want to stay here, you don't touch him, got it? One day there's going to be a cure for this, and when that day comes, I'll carry Justin across the country if I have to to get it to him."

Bill and Addy looked at each other, then Bill smiled. "Reasonable enough. What father wouldn't?"

****

They set out early in the morning, before the sun had risen. Going down the mountain was easy; gravity did most of the work. Both men carried empty backpacks, and Hoyt carried a shotgun and a rifle.

"I can carry one of those," Bill said. "If they get heavy."

"How many rounds you got in that revolver?"

"Three."

Hoyt stepped over a tree root arching up out of the ground, and pointed down at it to make sure Bill noticed. "There's a gun shop in town, we can hit it up before we leave."

The sun had risen by the time they reached the outskirts of town, with a few homes and even a strip mall dotting the roads before the hills had even leveled out. "Town's been encroaching on the mountain for years," Hoyt said. "Convenient for sure, but I always feared the day I'd see a Starbucks in my front yard. Guess I have bigger problems now, though."

"Hoyt, should we really be talking? We're in town now."

"Never seen any of them this high up," Hoyt said. "The hills trip them up, they spend most their time falling back down. Still, I guess a little caution couldn't hurt."

They crept among quiet houses and eventually little shops. Somewhere up the mountain a bird cawed repeatedly. Hoyt crouched behind a dumpster next to a shop, Bill crouched behind him, and Hoyt pointed catty-corner across the street. "There's the drug store. Might want to pop in and grab some Tylenol and Neosporin. Couldn't hurt to get some peroxide, too."

Hoyt stayed crouched as he crossed the road, then crept along the storefronts toward the drug store. Bill followed closely behind. Hoyt turned the doorknob of the drug store and the door creaked open. He raised his shotgun and swept the room with it as he entered, then he stood upright and walked further into the store. Hoyt went straight for the supplies he'd mentioned, but Bill stood still, mostly looking around. Hoyt stopped packing his bag and looked at him. "You don't need my permission, if you see something useful, take it. And close the damn door."

"Right. Sorry." Bill closed the door gently and then headed into the aisles.

When they finished grabbing what they needed, they headed back outside and down the street. Hoyt stopped beside a building, then muttered, "Shit."

"What?"

"That's the gun shop. The one with two of them outside."

Bill looked where Hoyt was pointing and saw a small brick building with two zombies wandering around near the front door. Heavy bars covered the windows, but he could still make out a small handmade sign that read *OPEN* in what looked like permanent marker, somewhat faded from years of facing the sun.

"Maybe we can go around to the back?" Bill said.

"I haven't tried the back," Hoyt replied. "Might be locked. Might even set off an alarm. We can get through town if we keep quiet, but you fire a gun or set off an alarm, and every one of those bastards for miles will come looking."

"Can we hit up the grocery store first then? Maybe they'll be gone by the time we get back."

Hoyt shrugged. "Worth a shot. This way." He led them behind a house, over a few fences, and eventually into the small back lot of a grocery store. One of the windows was broken, with a gaping chunk of glass missing, but jagged shards clung to the frame on the top and one side. Hoyt stopped them near the broken window.

"This place isn't empty," Hoyt whispered. "I've been here three times, there are only a few of them wandering around. As long as we stay quiet and stay low, we can get in and out with no problems."

He took off his backpack, put it on the ground inside the store, then climbed in, taking care to avoid the edges of the glass. Bill handed his backpack through to Hoyt, then wriggled in himself.

Hoyt crept down an aisle, waited as a nearby zombie shuffled back and forth, then headed into the next aisle when it turned around. Bill followed, mindful of his backpack so he wouldn't knock anything over. Hoyt grabbed a gigantic can of coffee and put it in the main compartment of his backpack, then handed another to Bill, who did the same.

Bill followed Hoyt through the store. The man was a master of sneaking, and knew exactly what he needed and where to find it. He didn't grab a lot; there was the coffee, toothpaste and a handful of toothbrushes, more over-the-counter medicine, gauze strips, glue, and matches. Bill grabbed some of each of them, except the glue, but he picked up some chamomile tea. Eventually Hoyt led him back to the window, then out into the streets.

They crept back across town, and Hoyt peered around a corner. "Gambled and lost. Now there's four."

"Let's try the back," Bill said. "If we can't get in, we can just head back to your place without the ammo."

Hoyt nodded. "If we trip an alarm, just get in and get your ammo as fast as you can. And whether we get in or not, you'd best be ready to follow me back home quickly. No tripping or getting lost. He pointed down the street. "See that bus? It'll cover us most of the way across the road." He crept toward it, waited for a good moment, then rushed halfway across the street and behind the bus, out of sight of the zombies. One turned their way as soon as Hoyt was behind it, and Bill peered around the corner, watching for it to turn back around. For a long time it didn't move, and Bill thought about motioning for Hoyt to go on ahead, but then the zombie spun around, and Bill headed across to the bus.

For the first time in a while they could walk upright without fear of being seen, and Bill and Hoyt savored the opportunity to stretch their limbs. Once they were on the opposing sidewalk, they were back to crouching, keeping behind the shops and houses, which were mixed in with each other indiscriminately. Finally they came to the back of the gun shop."

Hoyt winced and turned the knob, but nothing happened. No alarm rang out, but the door didn't open, either.

"Locked?" Bill said.

Hoyt nodded. The two men sat there thinking for a moment, until they were interrupted by a loud "Gah!"

Both turned to see a zombie approaching from around the corner of the shop next door.

"Guess we're doing this the hard way," Hoyt said. "Just try to get inside, most of them can't open doors!"

Hoyt led Bill along the side of the building, then around the corner. Two of the zombies out front spotted them, and groaned and hissed as they approached, which drew the attention of the other two zombies. "Inside!" Hoyt shouted, and sprinted across the storefront. He flung the door open and went in, and Bill followed just behind. He turned to shut the door, but a zombie got halfway in. Bill pushed with both arms outstretched, his whole weight on the door, keeping the zombie from getting in any farther.

Hoyt grabbed a rifle from where it was mounted on the wall and shoved the butt end of it at the zombie. The zombies pushing and shoving behind it kept it from moving any farther out the door.

"Not working!" Bill said.

"One second," Hoyt replied. He ran across the store, hopped over the counter, and grabbed a box of ammo. He came back to the front door, knelt down and took a match from his backpack, struck it, and lit the box on fire. Hoyt waited for the flame to take hold, then threw the box over the zombies, out of the shop, where it landed in the street. A few seconds later a loud *pop!* rang out, followed by another, then another, like fireworks. One by one the zombies turned toward it, more interested in the noise behind them than the hard-to-reach meals before them, and wandered toward the sound. Finally the zombie in the door slid out of the shop, and Bill shut the door behind him.

"Close call," Bill said. "Nice trick."

"Thanks," Hoyt said. "Let's hurry, that sound will draw even more of the fuckers."

The two men split up to get their ammo. Bill grabbed several boxes marked ".38 Special" while Bill picked up ammo for his shotgun, his rifle, a few .38s of his own, and some 9mm ammo.

Bill took a bow from the wall and a few packets of arrows.

"You any good with that?" Hoyt asked.

"No idea," Bill said. "But ammo won't last forever. Now might be a good time to start practicing."

Hoyt shrugged and grabbed two bows for himself, and more arrows. "Okay," he said. "Let's get the hell out. We can leave through the back, and make sure we leave it unlocked."

****

Bill entered the living room, which glowed from the light of the fire. He had just finished tucking Samantha in. Addy was sitting on the couch across from Hoyt in his big red recliner, and both of them had a mug full of tea before them. A third had been set on the table in front of the couch, still smoking warm, and Bill took his seat and lifted the mug to his mouth.

"All right," Hoyt said. "Let's talk about the thing that's on all our minds: How long you're going to stay here."

Bill swallowed his tea and set the mug down. "We don't want to impose," he said. "Just a night or two—"

Hoyt waved his hand in the air like he was wiping away Bill's words. "Truth be told, today's supply run was the fastest I've ever had. Maybe not the safest, but definitely not the most dangerous. And Lord knows I have the room and could use the company. You all are welcome to stay as long as you like, and I mean that."

"We couldn't ask you to give us your home," Addy said.

"I'm not," Hoyt said. "I'm asking you to stay in it with me. There's as much in it for me as for you. I grow crops up here, enough to feed me most the year, but just barely. You help me with the farm and more supply runs, we all keep each other safe, and we just might live to see the end of this thing."

"We're grateful," Bill said. "We really are. And we'll take a few days to think it over, if that's okay with you."

"Take all the time you need," Hoyt said. "If nothing else, let me know a few days before if you plan on leaving. We can head back into town and get you all some new clothes. I imagine some of Justin's will fit your girl well enough, but me and my wife were bigger than the two of you, so unless you want to hit the trail in baggy clothes, you'll at least want something from town."

"Deal," Bill said. He and Hoyt shook again, and Hoyt stood and raised his mug. "Good call on the tea. Not the best taste, but it warms the soul. Come on, I'll show you to one of the guest bedrooms. Never thought I'd actually use them, but Helen insisted on keeping them. Guess I'm glad she did."

****

A few days stretched into a few weeks, and one day Hoyt woke Bill early to take him into town to get new clothes. He didn't have to ask Bill if the Moores were planning on staying; the family fit into Hoyt's life like a slipper. Everyone knew they would stay.

Hoyt showed them how to farm, where to plant the crops so they'd catch the most sunlight, which ones to plant first and which ones could wait a while. He quadrupled the size of his garden, and at the end of one particularly long day, he stood over the plots of freshly tilled land while the sky turned red and the trees clattered together in the wind.

"What's on your mind, Hoyt?" Bill said. Hoyt didn't know how long he'd been there.

"Just hoping it's enough. I hunt, but my freezer doesn't fit much, so I have to cook everything pretty much immediately. Sure would be helpful if we could store shit longer."

"Freezer?"

"I have a little cooler I keep outside. Except for the summer, nights are pretty damn cold up here. In the winter I pack it with snow and ice. I only have the one though, and it's not big enough for deer, just rabbits mostly."

"We could get something bigger from town."

"One step ahead of you." Hoyt beckoned Bill over, then pointed down the mountain. "See that building there? With the green roof? That little shop's got a big ass metal freezer right outside. It's perfect, only it's far as hell, too far to be hauling deer."

"We could bring it up here," Bill said. "Look how close it is."

Hoyt smiled. "I like your spirit. Always wanted to try, but by myself it's impossible. With a little help, though…"

"It'll be a lot of work. Probably take three of us. Is it on wheels?"

"No, but it can be, with a little welding."

"All right, let's do it. You have everything you need?"

"I do now," Hoyt said.

The next morning they rose early. While Hoyt set out some dog food, Bill and Addy snuck into Samantha's room and gently woke her, told her to stay inside and just try to sleep if she could, and they'd be back soon. After that the trio headed down the hill with a bag of Hoyt's tools.

The shop was a deli, and it was high enough up that it was abandoned when the world first went crazy, and remained empty now.

"Lift that side," Hoyt said.

"Is there anything in here?" Addy asked. She lifted the lid.

"I emptied it out a while back. Thought I might use it to store food. Only took one trip down here in the snow to realize that wasn't going to work."

Hoyt had brought some heavy-duty casters he'd bought for a shelf he never finished, and while Addy and Bill lifted one side of the freezer, he welded the wheels to the bottom with a blowtorch. It only took a few minutes, then the couple lifted the other side. Bill watched anxiously for zombies, but Hoyt appeared to be right; they didn't seem to make it this far up the mountain.

"All right, set her down," Hoyt said. "Let's give those a minute to cool off."

They sat breathing in the cold air, letting it kiss their sweat away. "I hope Sammy's okay," Addy said.

"She's probably still sleeping," Bill replied. "Let's get back."

They rolled the freezer toward the trail, and from there it was slow going. The hill wasn't too steep, but the freezer had wheels, and gravity pulled on it, like the freezer wanted to run away back to its deli shop. Addy pulled from the front while Hoyt and Bill pushed from behind, and when they came to a snag or a root Bill would cross to the front, help Addy lift the freezer over and set the wheels down on the other side, then Bill would go to the back and do the same for the back wheels. It took them hours, but around noon they were on the trails surrounding Hoyt's house.

"There," Hoyt said. He panted a few times, wiped the sweat from his face, then pointed. "Right against the side of the house, where it's shady. The sun'll be off it almost the whole year."

They wheeled the freezer into place, then stepped back to admire their work.

"This is just the beginning," Addy said. "We really can make this place work."

"She's never let me down before," Hoyt said. "Things are getting better by the day."

"Mommy?" Samantha peeked out from around the house. "I heard you coming back. I didn't know if it was okay to come out."

Addy kneeled and hugged her daughter. "As long as we're here, it's safe," she said. "Just don't ever go near the shed, okay?"

"Okay. What's that?"

"It's a freezer," Bill said. "For storing food in the winter. Listen, why don't you and Mommy go inside? I have something I need to talk to Hoyt about."

Addy eyed Bill, one eyebrow raised slightly, like she was afraid. Bill just nodded, and Addy took Samantha's hand and led her inside.

"What's on your mind, Bill?" Hoyt asked.

"It's something I probably should've mentioned before. I kept meaning to, it just never seemed like a good time."

"I'm listening now."

"It's about Justin… There's a way to turn him back, Hoyt."

Hoyt stared into Bill's eyes, pierced his soul, and Bill knew his next words were crucial. "It's not a cure, per se. It's not permanent."

"But I could have him back, I could have *my son* back? And you didn't tell me?"

"It's complicated. Hear me out, Hoyt. You know getting bitten turns you into one of them. Well, it works in reverse. If you bite them, they turn back."

"What's the catch, Bill?"

"If you bite one of them, *you* turn."

Hoyt raised his head slightly, his eyes darted back and forth. "So if I bite Justin, he'll come back, but then I'll turn?"

"Yeah."

"No way of stopping that?"

"No. Not that I know of. We've met people before, some of them wander around finding zombies to turn back into people, and they travel in groups so they can keep changing each other back. It's not efficient, but it works."

"We can do that for him," Hoyt said, nodding toward the shed. "We have to."

"I think it would be better if we found a turning party, Hoyt."

"No one's been through here. Only you."

"We saw the smoke, someone else could. Or we could go to *them*."

Hoyt pounded a fist against the side of his house, and Bill flinched. "I don't think you understand what you're telling me, Bill. You're saying I could see my son today, he could be my son again *today*, but you want me to wait."

"There's no way to tell how long it'll take him or whoever bites him to turn. If we start that process now, we'll all be watching our backs until a turning party shows up. That means sleep shifts, it means taking time away from the crops, it means no more supply runs. Samantha and Justin can't bear that responsibility, it has to be us adults. There are only three of us. So much can go wrong."

Hoyt brought his fist back and let loose. Addy gasped from the side—Hoyt hadn't noticed her come back out—but it didn't matter. Hoyt's knuckles cracked hard against the side of his house, a few inches from Bill's head.

"You should've told me sooner, Bill."

"I was afraid you'd be mad, afraid you'd make us leave. I didn't want to risk taking my family back out there. You've seen what it's like in town, you haven't seen the bigger cities, the highways. We haven't been safe in years."

"I won't make you leave," Hoyt said. "But we're going to find us a turning party, and you're going to help."

"Absolutely. I'm sorry, Hoyt."

Hoyt sighed. "I've waited this long. I can wait a little longer. You're right, after all. I just… You should've told me."

"I didn't trust you yet. I do now, I have for a while."

"Then let's hope I can still trust you," Hoyt said, then he went inside.

****

In the morning Hoyt found Bill hovering over a map he'd spread out over the coffee table. "Morning, Hoyt. Come look at this."

Hoyt sat in his recliner and rubbed his eyes to clear them. "You have an idea where we can find a turning party?"

"I might. Here's us. This road cuts right between town and the city over here. Turners don't tend to go right into cities, but they do stay near them. They get a lot of work done around there. I bet if we walk up and down this road, we're sure to bump into one. They probably cut through here all the time."

Hoyt stood and headed for the kitchen. Bill followed him. "I've never seen anyone out there."

"How far out have you gone? All the stores we've been to were higher up. A turning party wouldn't come up this high unless they thought they had to. Too much work for no good reason. I put some coffee on already."

Hoyt poured himself a mug. "I have a little tent in the garage. We could camp out on that road a few nights. If we don't see anything, we come back here for a while, make sure everything's running smooth, then go camp out again."

"That's as good a plan as any," Bill said. "And we can do shifts. Addy's more than willing to help, so long as someone's always here with Samantha. I'd rather not risk her being out there again."

"That's reasonable," Hoyt said. He headed for his room.

"Where are you going?" Bill asked.

Hoyt turned to him. "To pack? We're leaving today."

"Oh. Okay, let me just get a few things ready."

They packed some extra clothes, food, some of the coffee, and the tent and blankets into two huge backpacks. With guns in hand, they met Addy and Samantha at the front door.

"You promise you're coming back, Daddy?"

"I'm coming back. We're just looking for more nice people like Mr. Reiner." Bill hugged Samantha, then moved on to Addy.

Hoyt kneeled down to Samantha's level. "Don't worry, kid. I'll bring your dad back safe. I swear it."

"Thanks."

"No problem, kiddo." Hoyt turned to Addy. "Hold down the fort for us, will you?" He leaned in closer, spoke quieter. "There's a revolver in the nightstand beside my bed, and the hunting rifle is mounted above the fireplace. Use them if you have to, but I don't suppose you will."

"Thanks, Hoyt," Addy said.

Hoyt and Bill stepped outside. Addy and Samantha stood in the door. "We're coming back with help for my son. Soon as we get him changed back to normal, you'll have a new friend around your age, Sammy."

"Won't that be nice?" Addy said. Samantha nodded, but there were tears in her eyes.

"Don't worry, Sam," Bill said. "I'm coming back."

****

They had snuck all the way down the hill through town and were walking beside the little road before Hoyt spoke. "I feel bad for pulling you from your family. I was still all bent out of shape."

"Don't worry about it," Bill said. "I shouldn't have kept that from you. Anyway, I wouldn't want you out here alone."

Hoyt grinned. "Already close enough to miss me?"

"You haven't taught us when to harvest the plants yet," Bill fired back. The two laughed, but after that they decided to save their breath for the walk.

They set up the tent in the grass by the side of the road. As it got dark, they lay beneath their blankets, only whispering from time to time.

"Wish I had something to do," Bill said. "Time's dragging on. Not tired yet."

"Can't risk using light," Hoyt said. "At all. Who knows what would see us. I just hope a turning party doesn't pass us up while we're sleeping."

"They would see the tent. They pay attention for that kind of thing. Any zombie they can turn easily. They'd definitely check out a tent."

"Maybe we should sleep in shifts anyway."

Bill shrugged. "I'll do it if you want to, but I think we'll be fine."

"Good," Hoyt said. "I'm tired as hell."

They were silent for a while as the world grew too dark to see anything, then Bill said, "Hoyt?"

"Yeah?"

"We'll get Justin back. I promise."

"...Yeah."

"Good night, Hoyt."

"Night, Bill."

****

Hoyt thought he heard something, and he realized his eyes were open and he was staring at the roof of the tent. Then he heard something for sure:

"Okay, okay, just take it easy."

He sat up and noticed the door of the tent was unzipped, and it was light outside. Hoyt crawled to the opening and saw Bill standing in the road with his hands up defensively.

"What are you doing out here?" someone asked.

"We're camping," Bill said. Hoyt quietly crossed the tent, grabbed his shotgun, and came out slowly, barrel-first, and stood and took aim at a man holding a pistol trained on Bill. To the man's left and right we're a woman and another young man.

"Andy," the woman said, and pointed toward Hoyt. The man with the gun looked Hoyt's way. He looked scared.

"Easy, now," Hoyt said. "What's all this about?"

"We're just passing through," Andy said.

"We're not going to stop you," Bill replied. "We're just camping out here, waiting for a turning party."

"Turning party?" the other young man said. "Which one of you is bitten?"

"Neither," Hoyt said.

"Who is?"

"None of your goddamn business."

The woman stepped between everyone and pressed down on the barrel of Andy's pistol, pointing it at the ground. "Enough! Look, Andy, they're clearly not bandits, one of them isn't even armed."

"Maybe we caught them off guard."

"Off guard?" Bill said. "We're practically sleeping in the middle of the road!"

Andy looked from Bill to Hoyt. "Yeah, well, no one said all bandits were smart." He holstered his gun, and Hoyt set his shotgun aside, then walked away into the brush a little to have his morning pee.

"Where are you all from?" Bill asked. "Have you seen a turning party?"

"Not recently," the young man said. We've been wandering for a while. We were with a little settlement, maybe four or five houses, but things went south there. One of the houses burned down, drew a bunch of zombies. Haven't seen anyone else since."

"Where was this?" Hoyt asked over his shoulder.

"Maybe fifteen miles east of here. Been walking ever since. It's slow going, especially around the city."

"We used to have a turning party come through monthly," the woman said. "Soon as they see what happened, they'll probably head out this way."

"That's good news," Bill said.

Hoyt returned to his shotgun and slung it over his back. "How long you think it'll be?"

The two young men looked at each other. "They stopped by two, maybe three days before the fire. I'd guess another few weeks before they come by where we used to be, another week or two to get up here."

"Shit."

"Wait, maybe you can help us," Bill said. "Hoyt, remember what I said about Justi—"

"Watch it, Bill."

"Yeah, sorry. Remember what I said? How we can't turn him with just the three of us?"

"Yeah, I remember, Bill."

Bill turned back to the trio. "How about we make a deal? We can offer you shelter, but you have to help us keep watch on each other until a turning party comes by."

"Now hold on," Hoyt said. "I'm not keen on other people opening my house up. Especially to people who had a gun on me."

"Come on, Hoyt, you'd have done the same in their shoes. How long has it been since you pointed a gun at *me*? This is perfect, Hoyt."

"Wait," Andy said. "No one said we *want* to stay with you."

"We have food," Bill replied. "A garden, we can hunt, we're safe, I promise."

"Come on," the woman said. "We need a place to stay."

Hoyt eyed the group. They exchanged glances, speaking with each other the secret language of people who have walked through hell together. "Can I at least get your names?"

"I'm Andy. This is my…" he turned to the other young man. "My husband, Zach."

"I'm Sarah," the woman said. "Zach's my brother."

"Andy, Zach, Sarah. Y'all know how to farm? How to hunt?"

"Sarah and I can fish," Zach said. "Our dad took us pretty much every weekend when we were kids. Don't know how you would store fish, though."

"We can store fish," Hoyt replied. "Can you shoot?"

"Well enough," Andy said. "Only have the one gun between the three of us."

Hoyt looked the trio over. He could tell they weren't lying from their worn shoes, torn clothes, dirty faces, and tired eyes. "All right. I have the room if you have the will. You stay with us, you have to contribute. Now my son, Justin, he ain't right. He's been bitten, long time ago now. If we change him back, are you three going to be willing to help? Just until we find a turning party?"

Andy, Zach, and Sarah exchanged glances. "Yeah," Zach said. "I guess so."

"Have any food on you right now?"

"We barely got out alive," Sarah said. "Didn't have much besides the clothes on our backs. We've been living off of whatever we find. Berries, came by a store that had some old cereal in it, but we're almost out of everything."

"Shit," Hoyt said.

"What?" Bill asked.

"Garden might not be big enough for four people, and we don't have time to plant more this year. Definitely don't have enough from last year to feed eight."

"We can get some fishing supplies from town. They can fish, you and I can start hunting."

"You ever hunt before, Bill?"

"No, but you'll show me, right?"

"Guess I'll have to. Okay, things'll be tight for a while, but we might be able to manage."

The trio helped them pack up their tent, and then they started back up the road.

****

"Sneaking through town might be hard with five people," Bill said.

"We'll find a way," Hoyt replied. "I always have."

"You sure you have room for all of us?" Zach asked.

"Got another guest bedroom, and I have a storage room I can clear out and put a bed in. I'd offer you Justin's room, but he's coming back. Anyway, if we run into any more people, we might just have to build another house."

"Can you do that?" Bill said.

"Never tried, but I imagine we could learn. Got the trees for it, got a hardware store in town we could get supplies from. Yeah, I imagine we could make something work. If we had to. For right now we want fishing and farming supplies."

"Wait, we aren't going to your house first?" Sarah asked.

"No point going all the way home and then coming back to town again. Might as well get our shit on the way."

The hardware store was on the far edge of town, close to the little road Hoyt and Bill had camped on. The front door was automatic and no longer worked, but they were able to slide it open with their hands, but it took a lot of effort, and the door rattled in its frame.

"Don't like being exposed," Hoyt whispered. "Let's be quick."

"We can slide it shut behind us," Andy said.

"Don't know if this place is clear. Might want to leave it open in case we have to bail. Just be quick and be quiet."

Hoyt and Bill left their bags by the door, as they were too big and too full to carry through the store. They crept through the aisles toward the gardening section, and already Hoyt could see a zombie wandering among the shelves as though it were perusing the flowers. Hoyt grabbed some jumper cables from a nearby shelf, snuck up behind the zombie, and then looped the cables over the zombie's head and between its jaws. The zombie lurched and flailed its arms above its head, but Hoyt held it steady.

"Get some hoes and seeds," he said.

"What kind?" Andy asked.

"Check the packet, grab anything that matures in about two months."

They gathered supplies into shopping bags, except for a few hoes and pruning shears, which Zach carried. When they were ready to leave, Hoyt shoved the zombie hard away from him, and the group fled the hardware store.

"Hoyt, we're carrying too much," Bill said. "Maybe we should just go."

"We just need the fishing gear," Hoyt replied. "I need dog food, but that'll have to wait, I guess. We got this."

"Fishing gear is in the gun store, right? That place was surrounded last time we came through."

Hoyt smiled. "Yeah, but last time we came through we unlocked the back door."

Inside the gun shop, Zach and Sarah picked out fishing gear while Andy stocked up on ammo. When everyone was stocked up to their weight in equipment, the five left the gun shop and started toward the trail that led to Hoyt's house on the mountain.

****

They shed their new belongings like old skin on the floor of Hoyt's living room. Tired, sweaty, and dirty, everyone collapsed around the room. Hoyt looked out the window at the setting sun.

"Guess we won't get to work today," he said. "Tomorrow I'll show you two the way to the stream."

"No running water?" Zach asked.

"No. We catch rain water for drinking and boil stream water for bathing. We have some stored up if the three of you want to wash yourselves. I'd be quick though, it'll be cold soon. Addy, can you show them where to find everything?"

"Yeah."

"Thanks. I'm tired as hell." Hoyt headed for his bedroom, and for the first time in a long time, he fell asleep not to the sound of chains in the shed, but of people talking and laughing in the other room.

The morning was quiet, except for shuffling outside. At first Hoyt assumed it was the wind shaking the trees, but it was too low, right outside his window. Hoyt grabbed the revolver from his nightstand and walked across the house. Sarah was sleeping on the couch, since they hadn't set up the extra room yet, so Hoyt was quiet not to wake her. He opened the front door with a creak, then went around to the side of the house.

A zombie was walking around, ankle-deep in leaves from last year. She was facing away from him, bumbling around near the shed. Inside, Justin rattled his chains. Then Hoyt saw the garden a few feet from where the zombie was wandering. With horror he realized the crops had been trampled, but from this far away, he couldn't see how badly.

Hoyt grabbed some rope from the basement, then went back outside. He snuck up behind the zombie, then slammed her against the shed. The metal clattered and clanged, and the zombie writhed and snarled, but Hoyt pressed his weight against her, keeping her from getting away. He pried the zombie's hands behind her back and wrapped the rope around them several times.

Bill and Addy came rushing out the front door. "Hoyt? What's going on?"

"Help me tie this bastard off," Hoyt said. He held the zombie still while Bill wrapped the rope around her feet, then they pulled, knocking the zombie over. After that they knotted the rope, successfully hogtying the creature, who rocked back and forth on her side.

"What's all the noise?" Samantha said from the door.

"Honey, stay inside," Addy replied. "Are there more out here?"

"Just the one, as far as I could see," Hoyt said. He was panting; he was too old for any of this. Hoyt forced himself to his feet. Sarah, Zach, and Andy had come out as well, but they stayed closer to the house, near Samantha. Hoyt went over to the garden. "Shit. Fuck, fuck, fuck."

"How much is salvageable?" Bill asked.

"I see one pepper untouched. Maybe a lettuce head or two. No tomatoes left, can't even find any damn beans. He must've been in there all night."

"Did she follow us up from town?" Andy asked.

"Must have. Shee-it. This is what I get for assuming we were safe up here. We should've had a higher fence, one they can't tip themselves over."

"Back in our settlement we had alarms," Zach said. "Just bottles and cans on strings, mostly. They'd rattle if anything came through."

"Remind me to get to making those," Hoyt said. "As soon as I figure out what the fuck we're all going to eat."

"We can still hunt and fish, right?" Sarah asked.

"There's not much game out here. We really needed those crops to carry us through the fall. You got any of that cereal left?"

"We finished it off last night. There wasn't a lot when you found us."

"Damn it. If we start hunting and fishing now, we might scrape enough together for all of us, but then we risk thinning the herd before winter's even set in."

"What about town?" Addy asked.

"Picked pretty well clean."

"Mommy?" Samantha said. Addy went to the house to comfort her daughter. The adults gathered in the yard, near the ravaged garden and the tied-up zombie still rocking back and forth and grunting at them. In the shed, Justin rattled his chains.

"And there's still Justin," Hoyt said. "Goddamnit. Eight people."

"We can make it," Bill said. "We'll have to ration it out, but we'll make it."

Hoyt shook his head. "We're talking maybe a rabbit every week, a deer every month if we're lucky. They don't come close, either, I have to go far out and wait, sometimes for days. In the snow."

"How are the fish?" Andy asked.

"I don't know, I haven't fished. I know they're in there, but no idea how many."

The banging and clanging from the shed was ceaseless, echoing across the metal walls of the shed, piercing into Hoyt's head and his heart, but suddenly everything was clear. "I have an idea, actually. You won't like it, but it'll get us all through the winter. And you won't even know you're hungry."

"What's your plan?" Bill asked.

Hoyt pointed at the shed. "Justin. He's been in that shed for years. Hasn't aged a day, hasn't starved—"

"You can't be serious," Zach said.

"If you just trust me—"

"We just met yesterday!"

"And already I've opened my house to you! I've fed you, I got you through town. We have to work together if we want to survive. As it is, there is one way, *one* way we all get through the winter, no questions asked. And that's by turning."

"Tell me he's crazy," Andy said to Bill. "Besides the dog food thing."

Bill was staring at the ground. "I don't know. It would work, I think."

"One versus eight," Hoyt said. "I know for a fact I can make it through the winter alone. I've done it more damn times than I can count. You let me turn all of you, I'll keep you in the shed, and sometime next year you wake up to a harvest big enough to get us through next winter easy. And that's if I don't find a turning party first."

"We'd be out for months," Zach said.

"And you wouldn't even know it."

"I don't know about this," Sarah said.

"I'm in," Addy said. She was standing a few feet away, holding Samantha's hand. "It's a good idea. We'd be safe from the cold, safe from hunger, it'd be like taking a long nap." She smiled at Hoyt. "And I trust Hoyt. If he says he's going to take care of us and wake us up as soon as he can, he's going to do it."

"If my wife is in, I'm in," Bill said. Hoyt put a hand on Bill's shoulder, and Bill nodded.

"I'm in," Sarah said. Zach and Andy turned to her. "Yesterday we didn't know if we would even survive to see the sunset. We could have a good thing here. Yeah, we fucked up a little, but we'll learn and we'll move on. This is the only way to guarantee our survival. It's the best case scenario, better than anything we've had so far. So I'm in."

"You're all crazy," Andy said. He sighed. "I don't have a better idea." He took Zach's hand, looked him in the eyes. "We're in."

Zach nodded. "Okay."

****

"Will it hurt?" Samantha asked.

Bill was crouched low so he was level with her. "Just a little pinch. After that, you'll fall asleep. That's all."

"You promise?"

"Yeah. And when we wake up, You'll get to meet Hoyt's son, Justin."

"You and Justin'll get along," Hoyt said. "I'm sure of it." He gave her his best smile.

Samantha hugged Bill. He held her tightly a moment, then stood up.. "Guess I'm going first, then."

Hoyt opened the door of the shed. Justin's chains jingled as he lurched forward, as close as he could to his potential meal. Hoyt moved in with the pliers; they had wrapped the ends of them in duct tape to soften then metal. He worked the end into Justin's mouth as carefully as he could. "All right, Bill. You're up."

Bill came forward, his arm held ahead of him. He took a look back at his family for courage, then looked forward and brought his arm within range of Justin's mouth. Justin bit down; Bill's arm bled, but Justin's teeth couldn't close because of the pliers. After a few seconds, Hoyt gently opened them, cranking Justin's mouth open and freeing Bill's arm.

"How is it?" Addy asked.

"Stings. Like getting a shot, kind of." He wrapped some gauze around the bite.

"Let's hurry this along," Hoyt said. "Hate to seem insensitive, but I don't know how long we've got, and we need to keep the zombies and the others separate until everyone's turned."

Zach and Andy came forward next, and they repeated the process. Sarah went after them, and then Addy brought Samantha forward. Samantha was crying.

"I won't let him bite too hard," Hoyt said. "I swear."

Samantha held her hand out. "Not like that," Addy said. "Your arm. You don't want him to get your fingers." She positioned Samantha's arm to show her, and then Justin bit down. Samantha started crying, and as soon as he saw blood, Hoyt opened Justin's mouth. Addy wrapped up Samantha's arm. "See?" she said. "Not so bad, right?"

"Of course n—not," Bill said from where he sat on the ground, his back against the wall of the shed. "Sammy's so brave. Come sit by daddy, Samantha."

Samantha went over to the wall of the shed and sat down beside him. Sarah sat next to her in case Bill turned.

"All right, Addy," Hoyt said. "Your turn."

Addy took her bite, and after prying Justin's mouth open for the last time, he stepped away. "Soon, Justin. Just wait a little longer." He started toward the door, then turned back. "And thanks. You've saved us all."

Near the door of the shed, Hoyt looked everyone over. "All right, we'll wait outside. When someone turns, the rest help me drag them into the shed and shut the door. Once you're all in, I'll lock the shed, and I'll wake you back up when I have enough food. And I'll keep looking for that turning party. Come on, everyone out."

"Think I'll stay," Bill replied. Addy's eyes filled with tears. "It's all right. I'm tired, that's all."

"Samantha, say goodnight to daddy."

Samantha hugged her father one last time, and then left the shed. Bill nodded to Hoyt, Hoyt nodded back, and then Bill's head drooped and rested against his chest.

****

"You with us, Bill? I should've known you'd be the last to wake."

Bill sat up. He was on the ground outside, it was a sunny day. He looked around and saw the shed behind him; Hoyt had taken tables and shelves and made a pen around the door of the shed. Suddenly Bill ran inside, and he saw piles of chains on the ground. He turned to Hoyt.

"He turned back this morning," Hoyt said. "Like I said, you were last."

Bill threw his arms around Hoyt. "It worked?"

"It worked. Come on, I'll show you all the changes I made."

The garden was twice as large as it was when Bill saw it last, with tomatoes and cucumbers, lettuce and peppers and all kinds of herbs and vegetables in various stages of ripeness, some Bill could pick and eat right away. Everyone was standing around the yard, and Bill found Addy and Samantha and took them both in the same hug.

"This here's Melissa." A young woman shook his hand. "She's new here."

"Hi," she said.

Bill's eyes widened. "Oh, is this the one that followed us up from town?"

"Yeah," Melissa said. "Sorry. About all the crops."

"Don't be sorry," Hoyt said. "If it weren't for you, we never would've come up with this plan."

Hoyt showed Bill the alarms he'd set up on all of the trails, cans strung up between the trees and shrubs. He pointed at the freezer. "There's still meat in there, I packed in with snow and ice from the winter.. We should keep an eye on the meat though, and never expect it won't turn."

"Yeah," Bill said. "Hoyt, where's Justin?"

Hoyt half-smiled. "He's inside. He's… a little shaken. But he'll be fine."

"Good. Hoyt… when you feel a little woozy… let me know. I'll bring you back. I swear."

Hoyt grinned widely, his teeth showing. "Of course you will. What the hell else do I keep you around for?" He looked over the others, then said, "Guess I'm about done here. I'm going to go spend the rest of the day with my son." He started toward the house, then paused. "Oh, and rest up. Tomorrow we get to work on planning a house. Nothing too fancy, just some extra room."

****

"Justin, you up, buddy?"

"I'm awake, Dad."

Hoyt sat at the foot of Justin's bed. "You can't stay in bed the rest of your life, Just. Don't you think you've slept long enough?"

Justin rolled over, away from him. "I don't feel like doing anything."

Hoyt put a hand on Justin's shoulder. "You'll feel better in a couple days, when we get you back to regular eating."

Justin didn't say anything. Hoyt sighed and stood up. "You need anything, you call for me." He started toward the door.

"Dad?"

"Yeah?"

"I feel like I don't belong here."

Hoyt sat back down. "What do you mean by that?"

"I feel wrong. I remember the shed. Lots of days and nights. You know that little girl?"

"Samantha? She's great. She's itching to make your acquaintance."

"We look the same age, Dad. But we're not. I was born in 1997. When was she born?"

Hoyt shrugged. "Early 2000s, I guess."

"Isn't that weird?"

"Weird?" Hoyt stretched out on Justin's bed. His feet dangled over the end. "You're not weird, Justin. Special, maybe. Not weird. And you're my son. You belong here. And I've missed you."

Justin rolled over and hugged Hoyt. "Dad, you... you're old. Your hair is grey now." Hoyt laughed, and Justin smiled. "I... remember you coming to talk to me. Maybe every day."

"Every day," Hoyt said. "I knew you'd come back to me someday. And yeah, I'm a little rough around the edges now, but I'm still here."

"I love you, Dad."

"I love you too, Justin." Hoyt sat up. "Get some rest, buddy. You'll feel better soon."

Justin covered up with his blanket, and Hoyt headed for the kitchen, where he lifted the bag of dog food and threw it in the trash. Then he saw it there, the cartoon dog staring up at him accusingly, and Hoyt took the bag back out, wrapped it around itself and sealed it with a rubber band, then put it in the cupboard in case he ended up adopting someone with a dog.

The After Life Part V: Another Day, Another Revolution

Brook woke to the sound of talking. She realized Ken had been talking for hours, but she could only remember bits and pieces. She sat up, and Ken stood from his salon chair.

"You still one of them?"

"No," Brook said. She rubbed her head. "I told you, biting them turns them back."

"Good," Ken said. "That means my plan will work."

"What plan?"

"Tell me how to get to my dad, and I'll tell you."

Brook sighed. "You feel sick? Having a hard time controlling your limbs?"

"No."

"Good, that means we have a while. If you feel anything like that, let me know."

"Why should I tell you anything? I haven't seen my dad in years, and you're hiding him—"

"I'm not hiding anything," Brook shouted, then lowered her voice. "Look, I can't just tell you how to get to him. The world outside this mall is a hellish nightmare world full of zombies if you're lucky and bandits if you're not. And I don't have a map with me, I just know the way, so if we're going to get to your dad, we have to do it together, okay?"

Ken sighed. "Can you tell me your name, at least?"

"Brook."

"Did my dad send you to find me?"

"No. Look, it's a long story, and trust me, I want to tell you everything, but we have a limited amount of time before you change back into one of them, so can I explain everything on the way?"

"How do I know you won't run off as soon as we get out of here?"

"Run off? Are you serious? I came in here to *get* you, why would I run off?"

Ken blushed. "Okay, yeah, that was dumb. All right, we'll help each other out, but you have to tell me everything."

"Start with your plan."

"Biting them changes them back, right?" Ken walked toward the front gate, where a dozen zombies were shoving and pawing and making guttural sounds. "We can just bite them as they stick their hands through. They'll all turn back, and we can all escape together."

"It… won't work like that."

"Why not?"

"They won't all change at the same time. And as soon as the zombies realize one of them isn't… *one of them*, they'll just eat them. Besides, sometimes it takes days to turn."

"Well, do you have any ideas?"

"Worst case scenario, my friends come for me and break us out of here. Well, that's not the worst case at all, really. Bandits might find us first. Or nobody will find us."

"You're just full of cheer," Ken said.

Brook hopped over the counter and joined him near the front. "I'm just trying to size up the situation." She looked over the zombies at the gate, then looked past them to get her bearings. "We could hang out behind the counter where they can't see us and hope they get bored and walk away, but I don't recommend it. That could take a while, and if we're going to be in here, we want to be on opposite sides of the counter when the other turns. Besides, that would spread them out, and I prefer knowing where they all are."

"All right, we'll put that in the 'maybe' pile then. Anything else?"

"I can make a lot of noise on the right side of the gate and keep them distracted while you squeeze out through the left."

"I like that even less," Ken said. "What would I do once I'm out? And how would you get out?"

"I'd need you to do the same. Distract them so I can sneak through."

"I don't like it. I don't think I can do it, I think I'll get us both killed."

"Ken, listen to me." Brook tried to look at him with confidence, but she was scared, too. "This is how things work now. There are no sure things, everything is a guess, every option is a risk. You have to make do with what you have, and try your hardest. We can do this, okay? As long as we work together. By tomorrow you'll be in Breathaven."

"Breathaven?"

"It's a town. The last one anyone knows of."

"That sounds like what someone who has no idea what to name a town would name a town."

"Yeah, well, you can thank your dad for that when we see him. Are you ready?"

"Ready? Wait, we're doing that plan?"

"Unless you come up with a better one. I'm going to draw them over here, you slide under the gate. Then just make as much noise as you can, and lead them to the right, got it? Just keep going that way, there's an escalator. Stairs give them trouble. Run up it, lure them up it, then come down the other side and come back here. I'll be out by then, and we'll head for the exit."

"Any way I can get you to swap our roles?"

"I fell from the upper floor earlier. I'm not sure I could make that run, let alone handle two flights of stairs. I don't really feel like finding out the hard way."

"Okay. You have any weapons or anything? You didn't bring a gun?"

"I don't have a gun, and if I did I wouldn't use it. These are still people, Ken. You were one of them earlier today. You really want to kill them?"

Ken looked at the vacant, writhing things on the other side of the gate. "No. They're just sick people, aren't they?"

"Yeah," Brook said. She smiled. "I wish your dad was that compassionate."

"What do you mean?"

Brook bit her lip. "I'll tell you later. You ready?"

"I guess."

Brook went to the far left side of the gate, then started jumping up and down and kicking the gate. "Hey! Over here! Look, free meal!"

The zombies slowly shuffled to the left side of the gate, pushing and scraping at the metal bars harder than ever. Ken kneeled down, lifted the gate a little higher, then got on his stomach and slid under it. He got to his feet as fast as he could, then started jogging down the aisle. He shouted and waved his arms, and one by one the zombies took notice and shambled after him. When they were all following, he ran faster, saw the escalator ahead, and went for it.

Halfway up the steps he saw a group of zombies at the top of the escalator. One noticed him, another noticed it heading for the escalator and followed, and Ken found himself two-thirds up the escalator, with zombies on both sides.

Ken hopped over the railing of the escalator and onto the adjacent one. The foot-wide gap between the two required a little stretch, but he landed on the other side and started down the escalator. The zombies followed, and some of them were already at the bottom. He turned and started up the escalator instead, leaning back to avoid the zombies reaching over the railing, and at the top of the escalator he jumped and shouted for their attention again.

When all of the zombies were most of the way up the escalator (and a few of them up it and now coming down his side), Ken ran down the steps and toward the little shop. Brook was waiting outside it, and when he was close, she turned and started down the walkway. Ken followed her as she weaved her way through the mall, taking wide routes around zombies, who would lunge or shamble after them, but never fast enough to get a bite in.

Finally Brook threw open a door, and the sunlight poured in. Ken raised his arms to cover his eyes, slowing to a crawl in the process. Brook took his hand and led him into the daylight while he shielded his eyes with his other.

"We can't stop," Brook said. "We're not safe just yet."

Ken's eyes adjusted halfway across the parking lot. There were rusted, abandoned cars, bits of clothing and garbage on the asphalt, and a few zombies limping toward them. Brook led him to the street opposite the mall, then into a back alley behind a store. At the far end of it a zombie was wandering back and forth, and there was a dead body sprawled on the ground about halfway down, but for the moment they were safe.

Brook sat down to catch her breath, and Ken did the same.

"All right," Ken said. "We're out. You owe me an explanation."

"Shh," Brook said. "Quieter. The streets are full of them." She got up and crept to the end of the building they were behind, then looked down the alley connecting it to the street. She motioned for Ken to follow, then crossed to the space behind the next store. "Your dad founded a town called Breathaven. People are safe there, for the most part."

Ken beamed with pride. "Should've known if anyone could save humanity, it would be my dad."

"It's not that simple. You and I are what people call 'normbies.' We're people who got turned into zombies, then got turned back. Your dad… he doesn't care for our kind so much." Ken stopped walking. Brook turned and looked at him. "We can't really afford to stop, Ken."

"He's my dad. You're telling me he hates me?"

"Warner lets normbies live in Breathaven, but he keeps us separate from everyone else. We get fewer rations, we have to live in buildings that are falling apart, we're not allowed to see humans without permission, and there are always armed guards watching us."

Ken just stared at her for a moment, as though he couldn't see the apocalypse around him, the skeletons of cars and shattered windows, but he could see only his pain, and he looked at her with betrayal, and for a moment Brook was afraid, until she realized that look wasn't for her. "Why?"

"He says it's about health concerns, keeping everyone safe, bullshit like that. I can't tell you why, I've never been within thirty feet of him. But that's what we're hoping you can do."

"We?"

"My friends. We sneak out and get food and supplies for the normbies. And we've been looking for you for years. We hope we can change Warner's mind about normbies, if he sees his own son is one of them. He needs to realize normbies aren't dangerous — we're just people who got a second chance, and he's taking that away from us."

"But what—" Ken started coughing, leaning forward to catch himself, then spat on the ground.

"We have to get going," Brook said. "If you turn, I'll bite you and try to keep us moving, but when I turn, you'll have to keep me somewhere safe until I can turn back and lead us home."

"Okay," Ken said.

They started down the alley again. Brook took off the hockey helmet and handed it to Ken. "It has a face mask. If you feel like you're about to turn, use it. That way you can't bite me."

They passed the body on the ground, and Brook slowed, staring at it, then shook her head and started moving.

"You know him, don't you?"

"He was my best friend. He died trying to find you."

"I… I'm sorry."

"It isn't your fault, Ken. Don't be sorry for things that happened while you were a zombie. Just make sure you do the right things while you're still in control."

They reached the zombie at the end of the alley. Brook shoved it, and it fell into some bushes. Brook and Ken rounded the corner, connected with the street, and started along it. After a while Brook slowed down, watching the side of the road.

"What—what are you looking for?"

Brook looked at Ken, checked his face for color. "We don't have much longer. I'm looking for a part in the grass, where we came through on our way in."

"You weren't kidding," Ken said. "There's a lot of guess work here."

"We can't exactly follow roads, it's too dangerous. It's better to walk through fields and follow rivers. We call it the wilderlands."

"Shit. It's like something from a movie." He made a *Gurk!* sound as he tried to stifle a cough.

"There." Brook pointed to a gap in the grass. They headed for it, and soon they were wading through an ocean of tall grass swaying in the wind.

After an hour of walking, Ken fell forward onto his hands and knees, trying not to throw up. His stomach was already empty, but it still pulsed like it wanted to clear out. His hands were trembling. Brook knelt beside him, put a hand on his shoulder.

"You haven't eaten in a long time," she said. "We'll get you some food back in town, but you have to start slow, okay? It'll be hard, but you have to go slow or you'll rupture your stomach. We don't have emergency rooms anymore."

"Okay."

Brook looked at the sky. "I think we should probably stop here for a while."

"Right in the field?"

"We should be okay. Sitting down, the grass covers us. Besides, more of my friends might be coming to meet us, it's important we stay on the path."

Ken nodded, then snapped the latch of the hockey helmet below his chin, lowered the face mask, and clicked it into place. He sat cross-legged on the soft, damp ground. "Did it rain?"

"It rained this morning."

"I haven't seen rain in a long time."

Brook smiled. "Let's hope you won't for just a little longer. That'll make it hard to see the path."

Ken convulsed, his head rocking back suddenly, then he regained himself. "Brook?"

"Yeah?"

"What if my dad doesn't care?"

"What—"

"What if it doesn't change his mind?"

"Whatever happens, we'll take care of you," Brook said. "We take care of each other."

"But I'm your last chance, right? What do we do about all the trouble he's causing?"

Brook ran a hand through her hair. "I won't lie, Ken. Things are getting… tense. Normbies are tired of being treated this way. There was a riot yesterday. Or was it the day before? I don't want any harm to come to your dad, but… The way things are going, people just can't take it anymore. We're starving, we don't have enough sound houses for when winter comes, and people are just tired of this."

"I'll do my best to convince him to change," Ken said. "I think I need to lay down."

"Go ahead," Brook said. "I'll do my best to keep us moving when you turn, but when I start to go, we'll have to stop."

"All right."

Ken lay down, shivering and trying not to cough. A half hour later, he wasn't moving at all. Brook waited, and then Ken sat up, slowly.

"Ken?"

"Ryeaaah…"

"Okay." Brook leaned in, raised Ken's pant leg, and bit down hard. He groped at her and tried to move his teeth, but the mask didn't give him much room. "Let's just hope you turn before I do."

Brook stood up, and Ken did as well. She started walking down the path, and Ken followed. A few times he straightened himself and almost walked away into the field, but Brook kept his attention.

With nothing around but grass, it was impossible to tell how far they'd gone, but Brook assumed it wasn't very far. She could already feel the shakes coming on, and an hour later, with the sun sinking lower in the sky, Brook stopped walking. Ken came at her, arms outstretched, but she only had to hold him away with one arm while he tried with no success to bite her through the mask.

Brook reached down and started pulling blades of grass out of the ground from the base, trying to keep the grass as thick and long as she could. She gathered several handfuls of it (sometimes needing to stop and shove Ken away so she could work), and then braided them together into a makeshift rope. It wasn't fit for climbing, but it might do the trick. Brook tied it under her jaw and over her head as tightly as she could, then tried opening and closing her mouth. She couldn't get her teeth more than a centimeter apart, but if she *really* tried… Brook made a second rope and tied it the same way, and then a third for good measure.

The coughs started, and Brook was worried she would cough hard enough to break the ropes, but they held. She made a few more and tied her feet together; if she turned before Ken did, her zombie would no doubt wander off with Ken's in tow, and she needed to keep them on the path.

At last she lay in the grass on the path. Ken's zombie kneeled down to feast, only pressing the face mask against her stomach and her arms and, at one point, her face, but altogether harmless. Then the zombie moved slowly, sluggishly, only pushing its face against her rather than biting, and then it rested its head on her stomach and lay still. Brook went out shortly after.

****

Brook woke in darkness to the sounds of grunting and groaning and the pain of a new bite in her leg. She sat up and saw Ken's zombie still trying to bite away at her through the mask. He must've turned again before she turned back. She bit Ken on the shoulder, then got up and started along the trail.

It was hard to see, and for a few seconds she wasn't sure whether the sun was rising or setting. She stopped walking long enough to get her bearings and figure out the sun was in the east; it was early morning. Ken's zombie bumped into her, and she started walking again.

The going was slow, but soon Ken's zombie fell to the ground and lay there. A few minutes later, Ken sat up, put a hand to his head, and felt the mask. He looked around. "Brook?"

"Everything's okay. We stayed in the field overnight."

"Have we moved at all?"

"A little. I feel fine now, I think we'll make it back to Breathaven before I turn again."

"Good," Ken said. He unlatched the hockey mask and peeled it from his head. His hair was matted and sweat dotted his face. "Think I'll just carry this for a while."

They started through the path in the grass, and eventually Brook saw a ring of rocks with ashes inside, the remains of their campfire from the other night. "Not much farther now, maybe two hours."

"What happens when we get back? About us turning, I mean."

"Breathaven has guards that change people back if need be, then they get put in a cell until a turning party comes by."

"Turning party?"

"Groups of people who go around turning zombies back into people. They turn each other along the way to keep themselves going. When they come by Breathaven every few weeks, they turn any zombies locked away there, then move on."

"Oh. ...And what happens when we get back?"

"I guess we'll talk to Dan Douglas. He's your dad's commander of the guard, but he's on our side. He'll take you to him."

"And then we just hope I can change his mind? Just like that? Minds are hard to change, Brook. Rome wasn't built in a day."

"We're not here to build," Brook said. "We're here to tear it down. Or just rearrange things a little. I don't know how your dad will respond, but…"

"But?"

"But I guess we'll find out."

Brook started to feel shaky as the river around Breathaven came into view. It wasn't enough to keep her from hopping across to the bus, but she knew she wouldn't last much longer.

Audrey was waiting by the gate, and she stood when she saw Brook approaching. "Oh my God. Is that him?"

"It's him," Brook said.

Tears formed in Audrey's eyes. "We couldn't send anyone. We were going to head out and meet you today, but we decided to stay here. Things have gotten worse."

They entered the alley between buildings and started toward the slums of Breathaven. "What do you mean?"

"Warner was going to execute Peter for attacking him. He made this big public display of it, then called it off at the last minute. The humans fell for it, but the normbies… they're pissed. Some are talking about open revolt now. Brook… we won't survive another riot."

"We won't need to," Brook said. "Let's go see Earl and let him know."

Brook, Ken, and Audrey walked the streets toward the abandoned coffee shop. Kids with sunken faces stared at them, a man with a blanket over his lap sat against the wall of a building that was missing most of its top half. "Brook! It's so good to see you. Have you brought any food?"

"Not today, Mr. Huang. But if everything goes as planned, we won't ever be hungry again."

They reached the coffeeshop and Brook knocked on the door.

"Who's there?"

"Brook, Audrey, and Kenneth Warner."

The door clicked and the teenage boy from before opened it. "You found him? You actually—"

"Where's Earl?" Audrey asked.

"Inside."

They entered the shop, and Brook thanked the doorkeeper as she passed. In the main room, Earl was sitting at a table looking over various papers, documents, and maps. He stood when they entered. "Is that—"

"Ken Warner," Brook said. "We're about to go see his dad."

"Is that so?" Earl rounded the table and looked Ken up and down. "And what are you going to say to him?"

"I'm going to ask him to stop," Ken said. "Brook told me all about what goes on around here. I didn't want to believe it, but I saw the town on my way in. I just… It's hard to believe my dad could do this. He's not himself. I'll talk to him."

"What if he doesn't understand?"

"I'll make him understand."

Earl smiled. "Good. You strike me as a good kid, Warner. I'm so sorry." Earl pulled a knife from his jacket, grabbed Ken by the shirt and yanked him toward him, then put the knife to his throat.

"Earl, what the fuck are you doing?" Brook shouted.

"This is how this works. This is how it was always going to work. You think a man like Hugh Warner is going to change his mind just because he sees a son he hasn't seen in years? You think he's going to take one look at this kid and change all this!" Earl motioned around them with the knife. "The only way to change Hugh Warner's mind is to make him realize he'll lose his son again otherwise."

"God damn it Earl, don't blow this for us now!" Audrey said.

"I'm not going to hurt him, I'm just going to show Warner that I can."

"Take it easy," Ken said. "This isn't necessary, I'll go with you willingly. You're right." Brook looked at Ken, and he stared back at her. "You're right about everything. My dad isn't going to undo years of damage overnight."

Earl relaxed his arm a little, but kept the end of the blade touching Ken's neck. "You're far more understanding than him, I can see that. I'm sorry, I really am. I hope worse doesn't come to worse, here. Audrey, get the door for us."

"Fuck you, Earl."

"Don't make me hurt him. Maybe showing up a little bloody will help drive the point home."

"No, that's a good idea," Ken said. He turned his head a little to make a tiny cut on his neck. A bead of blood dribbled down. "You've really thought this through. Only…" Ken coughed loudly and started convulsing. Earl fought to hold him still without stabbing him. "Sorry. It's just Brook and I had to keep each other regular on the way here. I'm worried I'll turn any minute."

Earl pointed the knife at Brook, not threatening, but because his other hand was around Ken's shoulders. "That true? Is he about to turn?"

Ken sank his teeth into Earl's arm. Earl screamed, dropping the knife as blood pooled through his sleeve. Audrey dove forward and grabbed the knife, then held it up to Earl as Ken ripped free of him. Earl raised his hands.

"Come on, Ken," Brook said.

"Find Dan," Audrey said. "He'll take you to Warner."

"You're making a mistake!" Earl said. "This is our only chance!"

"I know," Brook said. "But I'd rather keep Warner around than put you in his place. Warner could've killed Peter, but he didn't. Would you have let Ken go so easily?"

Earl shook his head. "He only did that to garner sympathy for himself."

"You're right. He was never going to kill Peter at all. What does that say about you, Earl?"

Earl grinned. "Fine then. Do things your way, Brook. I hope it works, I do, but it won't. In an hour you'll see, but by then it'll be too late."

"In an hour we'll be free," Brook said. "And we'll do it without killing anyone."

"You're wrong. You're so wrong. I just wish I had raised you better."

"You raised me just fine, Earl. I'll see you soon, when I walk through that gate with no guns pointed at me." Brook took Ken's hand and led him toward the door. The doorkeeper hesitated, then opened it and stood aside, letting them out into the day.

They found Dan on top of the gate between the two sides of town, and he came down as fast as he could. "Tell me that's who I think it is," he said.

"It is," Brook replied.

"Okay. Stay close by me, all right? I'll get you to Hugh's office, but if anyone sees us... Just don't let anyone see you, okay?"

He brought them to a door beside the gate, unlocked it, and looked around inside. He held up a finger to tell them to wait, then went in and motioned for them to follow.

They hurried down a little hall, and then Dan ducked into a small, unused room. He left the door open a crack and crouched by the wall next to it, and Brook and Ken crouched beside him. Brook struggled to control her legs from shaking too much, and covered her mouth with both hands to stifle a cough.

"You okay?" Ken asked.

Brook nodded.

"Let's go," Dan said. The two of them followed him into the hall, around a corner, and down another hall. Dan rounded the corner and bumped into another guard, almost knocking him down.

"What the fuck, Douglas?" the guard said. He looked at Brook and Ken. "What the fuck are normbies doing in here?"

"I'm taking them to confinement, Cohen," Dan said.

"Confinement's that way." He motioned down the hall, then put one hand on his sidearm.

"Yeah," Dan said, then head-butted Cohen, who fell onto his back. Dan crouched over him and put both hands on Cohen's sidearm so he couldn't draw it. "Warner's office is the one at the end of the hall."

"Help!" Cohen screamed, and Dan drew his baton and shoved it between Cohen's teeth.

"Go! Lock the door behind you!"

Brook and Ken ran past the two struggling guards, toward the office at the end of the hall. They reached it, flung the door open, and slammed it shut behind them. Brook slid the deadbolt into place.

Hugh Warner was standing, his eyebrows raised, his hand on the drawer of his desk. For a second Brook thought he'd pull a gun from the drawer and end their revolution right there, but he wasn't moving.

"Hey, Dad," Ken said.

"Ken? How did… Oh my God." Warner came out from behind the desk and wrapped his arms around his son, cried into his shoulder. "I missed you so much."

Ken hugged his father. "I missed you too, Dad."

"Your mother, she didn't make it. I'm so sorry."

"I know, Dad. It's okay, I know you did everything you could."

Brook's hands were shaking. "Ken?"

Warner pried his face from his son's shoulder, then looked at Brook. "A normbie? What the hell is going on?"

"Dad, this is Brook. She found me out there, in the mall where I got bitten. And she brought me home, to you."

Warner looked at Brook, then at Ken, then at Brook again. He held out his hand. Brook stared at it for a second, then took it and shook.

"You have my thanks for returning my son to me. I mean no offense, but can you go back home now? Give me and my son some time?"

"That's just it, Dad," Ken said. "We came here to talk to you about all of this. About Breathaven."

"What's there to talk about?"

"You have to get rid of that gate. You have to stop separating people."

"Ken, I can't do that. There's a health risk—"

"I'm one of them, Dad. Am I a health risk? Are you going to lock me out, keep me a few blocks away?"

Warner looked at Ken, then he looked at Brook with fury in his eyes. "You two have no idea what you're doing. You're going to undo years of hard work. There's a system in place, it can't change—"

"It will change," Brook said. "You're going to change it."

Ken looked at his son. He held only anger for Brook, but when he looked at Ken he only looked betrayed. "No one has to know," he said. "No one will know you're a normbie. I'll tell them you were never bitten, we were only separated, there was so much chaos."

Ken grimaced. "I won't do that, Dad."

"You can live uptown, with me. It'll be like you were never gone. Don't—don't do this to me, Ken. Don't take this from me."

Ken's eyes twitched, trying to keep clear from the tears. "Dad—"

"I love you, Ken. These people, these normbies… do you know what they'll do to me? They'll hunt me down, they'll kill me, all of us."

"We won't," Brook said.

"They would never," Ken replied.

"You're going to trust them? Someone you just met? You're a tool to them, son. You're a pawn sent to checkmate the opponent's king."

Ken looked at Brook, then at his dad. Brook realized he was slipping away from her. She tried not to cough.

"Dad… where were you?"

"What do you mean?"

"I was in that mall for years. No one ever came for me." He turned to Brook. "Except for her. A total stranger." He turned back and met his father's eyes. "Where were you?"

"I searched, I did. I sent out parties, but we didn't know where you were."

"He's l—lying," Brook said. "He's how I knew where to find you."

"Don't listen to her, she's using you!"

"She saved me, Dad."

Hugh Warner put both hands on his head and crouched down. He let out a sob, then began crying loudly.

"Ken," Brook said, "I'm gonna turn."

Ken handed Brook the hockey helmet, and she put it on and lowered the mask. "Dad," Ken said. "This doesn't have to hurt. All you have to do is let go."

"You make it sound so easy, Ken."

"It *is* easy. How long did it take you to let go of me? And now here I am. This is a second chance, dad. That's what normbies are. Don't, don't let me go again, Dad. Not when I'm standing right in front of you."

Hugh Warner burst into tears. He stood and hugged his son again, sobbing into his shoulder. Brook collapsed to the ground. Ken hugged his dad.

"Dad… please."

Brook stood again, moaning loudly.

"You see, Ken? You see what they are? What they could turn us all into?"

"Don't look at her, Dad. Look at me. I'm no monster."

"You want to throw in with them?" Brook's zombie approached, and Hugh shoved her as hard as he could, throwing her to the ground. "Fine, you can be with them. You'll live downtown with the others.

"Dad, please—"

"Take her and get out of my office."

"Dad," Ken said. Brook's zombie was standing up again, and Ken grabbed her by the shoulders and held her, facing away from him, while she gnashed her teeth beneath the mask. "Dad… you're more of a monster than she could ever be." Ken tore the mask from Brook's head and shoved her at his father. Hugh Warner screamed and put his hands up, and Brook's teeth clamped into his arm as they fell to the ground. She bit into it again and again, and blood dripped from Warner's arms to the floor.

Ken grabbed Brook and pulled her from his dad, shoved the hockey mask over her head, and latched it. He held Brook steady.

"What have you done?" Hugh cried. "You son of a bitch. What have you done to me?"

"You're one of us now too, Dad."

"I won't turn! I'll never be one of you!"

Warner rolled onto his side, curled up, and cried. Ken lay Brook on the ground, put a chair over her so it would take a minute for her to wriggle free, and kneeled beside his dad.

"I love you, Dad."

"How could you do it…"

"Because I love you."

Hugh looked up into his son's eyes, tears streaming down his face, blood streaming down his arms. He nodded, slowly. "Okay," he said. "Okay. But what if they won't listen to me?"

"You called yourself a king. You made them listen before, you can do it again."

Ken helped his father up, then Hugh Warner walked to the door of his office and opened it. The hall was full of guards, Dan Douglas with his back to the door, aiming his gun at all of them.

"Put that away," Warner said. The guards all stared at him, the blood dripping to the floor, the zombie approaching behind him. Warner turned and pointed at her. "Someone take her to confinement and have her bitten. When she's turned back, gather everyone in Town Square."

"Everyone from uptown?" a guard asked.

"Everyone," Warner replied. "And if I turn, turn me back. I have one last speech to give."

****

Brook sat up. She was in a small cell, the walls made of plywood, once a larger room now sectioned off into confinement cells. Soon the door opened, and Ken came in.

"Hey," he said. "I'm… sorry I made you do that."

Brook looked at the ground. "You kinda used me."

"I know. I didn't know what else to do."

Brook hugged him. "It worked, though. I think I can overlook it, just this once."

"Thanks," Ken said. "Let's go. My dad's waiting for you."

Ken and Brook headed through the halls, then to a door. Beyond it, Brook could hear Warner's muffled voice, giving one of his speeches. Ken opened the door into Town Square, where a large group had gathered.

"There they are now," Warner said. "My son and his friend, a young woman named Brook. Through their actions, I've learned that the threat from normbies has passed, and likely never existed at all. For these reasons, I am now lifting the segregation."

Most of the crowd cheered. A few booed. "We'll all starve!" someone shouted. "They'll turn us all!" another added.

"Then we'll turn each other back," Warner said. "It's only a matter of time before I myself turn. And we have plenty of food, plenty of shelter. We will be fine, as long as we take care of each other. I'll be happy to answer more questions."

Many of the people up front raised their hands. Earl came up beside Brook.

"I guess you did it after all. I'm here to eat my words. And apologize."

"Accepted," Brook said.

Earl grunted. "That was easier than I thought."

"I've been fighting for years. I'm not going to fan the flames now that they're finally out."

"I've never been more happy to be wrong," Earl said. "I just hope it lasts."

"I've ordered the gate torn down," Warner said. "It's the last order I'll give. I hereby turn governance of Breathaven over to my son, Ken Warner." Hugh searched the crowd, locked eyes with Ken, who was standing in the back, with Brook and the other normbies. "He's a better man than I ever was."

The crowd cheered as Warner left the stage, and many of them dispersed. Most of the normbies stood around town square, visiting their friends or talking to strangers.

Brook headed to the edge of Town Square, toward the gate. An old man sat on his porch, shotgun in hand. Brook walked up the steps toward him and stopped at the top. The man's grip tightened around his gun. Brook held out her hand.

The old man sighed, leaned his shotgun against the wall of his house, stood, and shook her hand. "There," he said. "You got what you wanted. Now get off my porch."

The After Word

A few of what I would consider my best ideas started out as speculative scenarios that grow like seeds, sprouting off into other ideas and concepts until I have something I can't let go of. Most of them end up getting used by someone else long before I ever do anything with them, and in ways more clever than I would have come up with.

Normbies is a rare exception where a simple idea—What if biting zombies turned them back into people?—sprouted into all kinds of different concepts and scenarios and ended up as a project I'm proud of.

It's sad to say that almost as soon as I had that initial thought, I realized someone somewhere would turn those who had been bitten and come back into second-class citizens, so that story arc ended up at the heart of the collection. But there were other aspects I had to visit with this new lens I'd made, from Americana to zombie fiction to that old '50's and '60's horror movie vibe, so a short story collection made more sense than a novel.

I wrote this one in the mid 2010's, one of the last prose works I actually finished. Once upon a time I tried to get it cleaned up and ready so my dad could read it before he passed, but I missed that mark. It's something I've come to terms with, and I find comfort in knowing that somewhere, somehow, he's reading it now, reading it before all of you get to. And it gives me hope that I'll write again someday. I wish I had never stopped.

But life gets in the way for a lot of us, in a lot of ways. Unlike the normbies in this book, we don't get a second chance, but balancing what we are and what we want to be is difficult enough without the literally life-threatening pressures of society and everyday life.

I think any point I could make here has probably been made already and been made better by someone else, so I guess I'll thank you for taking time out of this crazy, hectic, beautiful chaos we call life to read what I've written. It means a lot to me. Some days it's the only thing in the world that means anything to me.

But alas, life shambles on.

David J. Lovato
May 2022

Now You Can Normbie, Too!

I'm sure I'm not the only writer to come up with an idea that sounds amazing, and maybe even make some progress on it, only to find out it's been done before. Not in a general sense, but some specific aspect keeping the whole thing afloat, and when you tear it away, the whole ship sinks.

The concept behind this collection—a zombie apocalypse in which biting zombies turns them back into humans—is probably one of the better ideas I've had that, as far as I'm aware, nobody beat me to. I remember being excited when I wrote this collection, back in 2015 or so, and I'm even more excited now, publishing it in 2022.

One thing that remained consistent throughout the process was a sort of emptiness. I wrote the stories I wanted to for this collection, but it always felt like there could be more to this world. Try as I might, I wasn't able to come up with any more ideas I couldn't let go of.

So I found myself at the intersection of a problem and a solution. I decided I would create Normbies as a shared universe, one anyone is free to write within. Think the same concept as Lovecraft's Cthulhu Mythos, or Baum's Oz series, or Asimov's Foundation series.

The only stipulations as of this writing will be that anything published as part of the Normbies universe has to follow the rules set forth in this book, and involve characters other than the ones I've created. The idea is to have people more clever than me find those stories I couldn't. Give credit where it's due; I don't need royalties, but pointing readers back in the direction of the original work would be appreciated.

Other than that, have at it. Knock 'em dead out there.

About the Author

David J. Lovato was born in California in 1988. He spent his life moving around the United States, and currently resides in Missouri. You can keep up with him on his website: www.davidjlovato.com

Also by David J. Lovato:

Dark Things, a collection of four short stories.
Six and Seven, a novella.
The Ones Who Follow the Water, a novel.
The Forever Earth, a novella.
The Foreland, a novel.
The Afterglow, a novella.
This Can't Be All There Is, a poetry collection.

The Zombiemandias Series:

After the Bite, a collection. (Co-Authored with Seth Thomas.)
In the Lone and Level Sands, a novel. (Co-Authored with Seth Thomas.)
In the Year of Our Death, a novel.

The Pen and Paper, Wood and Nails Series:

Permanent Ink on Temporary Pages, a poetry collection.
A Means to an Ens, a collection of poems and photographs.
Build Yourself Better, a poetry collection.
Pen and Paper, Wood and Nails, a collection of the above three works.

Edited by David J. Lovato:

Crypto Bizarro: A Compendium of Obscure Horrors, an illustrated anthology. (Multiple authors, illustrated by Josh Leichliter.)

A Note About Reviews

Thank you for reading this book. Please consider leaving a review of it on Goodreads and/or the store where it was purchased. Reviews are crucial for authors, and a few moments of your time can go a long way. Thanks again for reading!

www.ingramcontent.com/pod-product-compliance
Lightning Source LLC
Chambersburg PA
CBHW021957120726
47992CB00001B/305